# DATE DUE

| | | |
|---|---|---|
| | | |
| | | |
| | | |
| | | |
| | | |
| | | |
| | | |
| | | |
| | | |
| | | |
| | | |
| | | |
| | | |
| | | |
| | | |
| | | |

# GRAVEL QUEEN

# GRAVEL QUEEN

## Tea Benduhn

SIMON & SCHUSTER BOOKS FOR YOUNG READERS
New York   London   Toronto   Sydney   Singapore

SIMON & SCHUSTER BOOKS FOR YOUNG READERS

An imprint of Simon & Schuster Children's Publishing Division

1230 Avenue of the Americas, New York, New York 10020

SIMON & SCHUSTER BOOKS FOR YOUNG READERS is a trademark of Simon & Schuster.

Book design by Greg Stadnyk

The text for this book is set in Photina.

Manufactured in the United States of America

10 9 8 7 6 5 4 3 2 1

Library of Congress Cataloging-in-Publication Data

Benduhn, Tea.

Gravel queen / Tea Benduhn.—1st ed.

p. cm.

Summary: All Aurin wants to do the summer before her senior year in high school is hang out with her friends Kenney and Fred, but when she falls in love with Neila, everything changes.

ISBN 0-689-84994-X

[1. Homosexuality—Fiction. 2. Lesbians—Fiction. 3. Friendship—Fiction.] I. Title.

PZ7.B43158 Gr 2003

[Fic]—dc21          2002003083

*For Martin and Samantha*

I'd like to thank the following people, in no particular order:

My editor, David Gale, and his assistant, Ellia Bisker; Lisa Jahn-Clough for her advice and wisdom; Myra McLarey, DeWitt Henry, and Terrence Laster; Lara Zeises, Steven Goldman and Laurie Stolarz for their detailed, significant and stellar attention; Claire Helgeson, Beth Keiser and Michael Strickland, without whom I would have never gone beyond college; Robyn Overstreet, Mary Theus, Elizabeth Valera, Becca Kirk, Jenn Grant, and Alicia Zander for their contributions to my life; Susan Nusser for "Tubercular Purr;" anyone else who has somehow supported me or my writing habit; and of course, my family.

# CONTENTS

# Glamour Girls

At the beginning of my movie, before the lights come up, you'll hear music. The audience will be primed for adventure-viewing because of the soundtrack, which will be provided mostly by folk-punk girl bands with names like "Eleanor's Sister" or "Tubercular Purr."

Lights out. A single guitar starts fast but low. Drums come in, sounding like they're being scratched with kitchen utensils. Bass picks up the beat, subsiding into the undercurrent. The music picks up speed with the crescendo, then plateaus when the singer comes in. Her voice is full of gravel and makes you want to reach down into her throat and pull up her voice to figure out how it works, or to swallow it yourself.

The dark screen begins to fade into image as the music rises. There's a round yellowish girl with dark hair driving a beat-up blue pickup truck with some rust around the fenders. That's me.

The red clay kicks up from my tires as I drive down the dirt road. You don't know yet whether I am going away from or toward something, but I guess I'm doing both. Maybe I just robbed a convenience store, or witnessed a murder. Maybe I'm going to join the circus to avoid a rotten uncle. No one knows at the beginning because you just see me driving. And I look so cool, with my cat-eye sunglasses on.

All the colors will be intense: bright yellow sun glinting off the dried raindrops crusted to the truck's dusty windows, saturated red dirt road, deep azure sky. It looks like a late summer afternoon; the trees have patches of lime green leaves and that curious golden quality to them that you only get on humid days.

A cloud of dust obscures the view for a moment, then pan to a huge brick house. A silhouette of someone blocking the sun stands at the edge of a manicured bright green lawn, waiting for me to pick her up. She tosses her bag into the back, and hops in.

Then we go.

Real life doesn't seem to be quite as cinematic.

"You're wearing *that?*" Kenney arches one of her meticulously plucked eyebrows at me.

I look down at my plaid sneakers and worn-out jean shorts. "What?"

My best friend: the nine-foot-tall toothpick with hair like fire. Of course she can't see the glory of my broken-in socks and comfortably relaxed yellow T-shirt. To her, these items are odious because there is no glamour involved. When she puts together an outfit, she chooses it based on its impact on the Richter scale.

Today, when she pulled up in front of my house in her Mary Kay pink vintage Mustang convertible, she made sure to toss her head *just so* as the boy watering the Johnson yard gaped at her lanky arms and long legs unfolding from her tiger-striped plush bucket seats.

And now she's standing in front of me wearing a knee-length red and white hounds' tooth skirt with a clingy bright red shirt, and pulling polyester printed items out of my closet and tossing them at my feet. Only Kenney can wear red with red hair and not look like tomato soup. As for me, I am convinced she keeps me around for my kooky-best-friend sidekick quality.

"Come on, Aurin, we can always do better." She puts her arm

around my shoulders and guides me toward the bathroom so I can change.

"Well, where are we going?" I ask as she shuts the door behind me and makes herself comfortable rummaging through my room.

"To the park to meet Fred."

"Big deal." I pull on the beige button-down dress with robin's egg blue flowers that she'd shoved at me.

"What if we see somebody?" Kenney asks. "You've always got to consider running into people."

I open the door and roll my eyes. "I don't see why I need to think about that. It isn't as if I'm ever going to have more than two friends anyway."

"We're going to be *seniors* in a few months, Aurin. Don't you want to reinvent yourself? We're not going to be in high school forever, you know. This is your time to be foxy. Use it well."

"Girl crap," I mutter.

"And what's with that hair-do, lady?" Kenney grimaces. "Who wears hankies on their head anymore?" She pulls the bandanna off of my head.

"I was just trying to get my hair out of my face."

"We can always do better." Her refrain. She grabs a bottle out of her purse and starts squirting my hair and crunching it into clumps. She digs through her bag some more, then starts poking bobby pins into my hair, styling it into a more organized mess.

Her hair, of course, is perfectly styled to match the '40s look she's been cultivating lately. Apparently she thinks we both need to fit into her old movie image, create *total illusion*. She doesn't appreciate the fact that I'm the director, not an actor. I don't know who I'm supposed to be trying to impress anyway.

Kenney rifles through my closet, "Here." She shoves a pair of old-lady shoes at me, the ones with a thick, short heel and square toe that I got for fifty cents and painted brown. She pauses and looks at me while I put on the shoes.

I shift my legs, scratching my knees against one another. Kenney is still considering the outcome of her fashion restructuring. A smile slides onto her face. "Now, Aurin, that is so much better! Just see how nice you look. Why don't you ever wear this?" She tugs at the corner of the dress, straightening the hemline.

"It's hot and itchy?" I offer.

Kenney glances at my watch—*she* never wears one. "It's getting late, we better go."

That's settled. And here we go to the park to meet Fred.

# Meow

Fred Wallace. We have known Fred for three years.
He moved here from Chicago, and still won't accept that he lives
in the South. He never misses a chance to remind us of how dull
and close-minded it is in Greens*boring*.

"Hey, kitty cats!" Fred is perched on the rail of the gazebo,
protruding from a hem of neatly trimmed hot pink azaleas.

Pretend for a moment that people are jewelry. If I'm topaz
and tiger's eye with my tanned skin and amber-lit eyes and hair,
he is diamonds and coal. He is made of pure carbon forms. Fred's
black hair and pale skin would look the same on either side of *The
Wizard of Oz*. And the smudge of stubble staining his chin would
probably cut your fingers if you tried to touch his face.

"You look stunningly fabulous." Fred and Kenney kiss cheeks
like they're French or something.

"And look at you, Miss Thang!" Fred pokes his chin into his
neck and struts around me making a short "mm-mmm" sound.
"And your hair all done up like you just haven't done a thing to it
all day."

I smirk. This part is true. Since the humidity just makes my
hair frizz, Kenney's teasing and spritzing make me look like I just
crawled out of the garbage dump.

"Big deal," I say. "We aren't *doing* anything."

"On the contrary, my little sourpuss munchkin friend. Look."
Fred points toward a group of guys playing Ultimate Frisbee. We
always hang out in the park, guy-watching from the playground,

which is secluded by trees. Grant Grayson is among them, and Fred is desperately in love with Grant. Okay, maybe not *love* exactly, since Grant doesn't even know any of us exist. But he would like to be in love with Grant.

Grant is the epitome of "guy." Nothing more to say there. He's a symbol. He's one of those guitar types—the same cool guy that everyone has a crush on at Shady Brook High.

"How many times do we have to do this same old scene?" I ask.

"Until we get it right," Fred tells me.

"You know, Aurin, if you're just going to be bitter, you can go home," Kenney says.

"You love my bitterness," I say. "It balances all of your happy-and-nice." I wrap my hand around the chain of a swing, and face the field.

"Whatever." Kenney flops down into the swing on the far left and examines her cuticles.

"Huh. Looks like there's a new guy out there." Fred says "guy" like it has quotation marks around it, and points toward the field.

In my movie, the sea of boys parts, and standing in the middle of them is angel music and sunshine. She is a girl with rosewood skin and a lion's mane of short, springy, bleached-yellow curls that bounce on top of her head. She trots, catching and tossing the Frisbee. All of the sound is dimmed around her, and everyone else is in shadow.

"I thought you didn't like girls." Kenney picks up on Fred's ability to note the encroaching threat to his territory on the playing field.

"I like the two of you," Fred returns. He sits in the middle swing and sways from side to side, alternately bumping into one or the other of us.

"You know what I mean." Kenney slaps him lightly on the shoulder.

"It doesn't hurt to look from to time, does it?" Fred adopts a gruff, butch voice. "I need to keep in practice, you know." He puffs out his chest like a football player. "Just in case."

"In case of what? In case all the men in the world die except for you?" Kenney asks.

"In case they don't make queers anymore," Fred says. "In case one day they just stop."

The two of them laugh while I squint and focus my eyes on the Frisbee players. She's the only girl out there. The way she runs so easily reminds me of horses, while the way the guys jostle into one another makes me think of dogs; they're a pack of dogs running around chewing on each other's faces over there.

"Hey, you guys," Kenney says.

"Yeah?" Fred and I respond as we must. Roll call.

"You know the community arts center? Well, they're having ballroom dancing classes this summer and open house is tomorrow. Let's go."

There is no question involved. Even if we didn't want to go, she would make us feel like shit for the next few days if we refused. Then she'd bring it up periodically for the rest of our lives. Sort of like, *remember when you wouldn't help me eat that burrito and I had to throw the rest of it out and then we saw a homeless guy and we couldn't give him our food because we threw it out because you wouldn't eat it?*

"I'll think about it," Fred says. I should note, he does not sound enthusiastic.

Kenney turns and narrows her spring grass green eyes at me. I shrug my shoulders. "I guess so. Lemme think about it too."

heart flops in its chest, falls into my shoes, and seeps out around my feet to follow her. "Got it!" she shouts to the group of eagerly waiting guys.

Kenney and Fred are breathless and laughing and getting closer.

"Hey, Grumpus." Kenney reaches her arm around from behind and pulls me back into her. She ruffles my hair like I'm her kid sister, then kisses the top of my head. "Did you get enough grouching done over here alone?"

"Ha ha," I say, flat-tone. "Very funny."

"What's up with you?" Fred says. "How come you're so gloomy?"

"How do you know what I'm feeling? I haven't even said anything."

"We can tell," Kenney says. She's alternately pulling each of her feet up behind her, stretching.

"What did we miss while we were gone?" Fred asks, now alert to the game again.

"Some guys tossing a Frisbee around. A lot of late-breaking news, I'm sure," Kenney says. Then she sighs loudly. "I'm bored. Let's go." She covers Fred's eyes with her hands while turning his head, then directs him toward the parking lot.

"Oh come on," Fred protests.

"No more," she says. "Let's go now."

I look behind me as we walk toward the parking lot, gravel crunching and spraying beneath our feet.

"Whatcha' lookin' at, Aurin? I thought you weren't interested in those guys," Kenney says.

"I'm not," I say.

# Me and Fred, Dancing

I hate dancing. I do not want to have anything to do with organized bodily movements that are unnatural to my own, dictated to and enforced upon me by someone criticizing the way I don't do it right because I can't feel the rhythm because it just isn't in my blood and bones. I want nothing to do with any of it at all.

Yet here is Kenney pushing me out my front door toward her car at ten o'clock on a Tuesday morning. In June.

"Come on, Aurin." Kenney is actually tugging on my arm. "It'll be fun—just like one of those old-timey movies."

I brush her hand off like a fly.

"You have to. It's the perfect thing for our '40s aesthetic. Besides, Fred's going to do it."

"What?" I stop walking and turn toward her.

Kenney walks ahead of me, around her car, and ducks her head for a moment to unlock the door. She looks back up at me, a devilish smile spreading across her face.

I sigh. Cross my arms. Shift my footing. I do not take another step toward that car.

"Come on!" She straightens back up and bounces a little on the balls of her feet, then stops. She reaches her lanky arms toward me above the car and holds them there for a moment with her head tilted a little back and to the side, her face pleasantly innocent and sincere: a graceful statue. Nurturing almost, motherly. She breaks pose and waves me in toward her car, the puppeteer becoming impatient.

I shake my head. "I don't think so."

Her shoulders collapse, the puppet's strings lax. "Pleeez." She puckers up her face, then pouts. Her head rolls around on her neck without direction.

"I can't dance."

"But they teach you. That's why it's called dance *lessons*. Besides, what are you going to do while Fred and I are having a blast, dancing?" She hops back around the car and loops her arm through the crook of my elbow. She wraps her other arm around my shoulder and guides me toward the car.

"I'll think of something, I'm sure." I pull the handle of the car door.

"I don't think so. In a few days, you'll be complaining about how bored you are. Kenney scoots back over to her side of the car.

"How did you get Fred to do it anyway?" I don't need to ask this question. I already know: Kenney's a grand convincer. I get in the car and pull the door shut, secure the belt.

"What do you think?" Kenney's eyes twinkle. "What queer guy doesn't want to be a dancer?" She engages the gearshift, and turns the ignition key.

"Kenney, that's ridiculous," I say.

She doesn't say anything.

"You're stereotyping people. Stereotyping *Fred*."

"Oh, give me a break." Kenney rolls her eyes and makes a *pfffw* sound. She backs the car up slightly, then shifts back into first and turns the wheel away from the curb.

"Well, he's Fred. I mean, we *know* him. He's our friend."

"Exactly." She presses the gas pedal and slides a CD into the player as we pull into the street.

She knows I love this song. I turn up the volume. The bass

starts in, sounding like the theme from a spy movie, and the singer's voice is a thick velvety plush carpet of deep smoky burgundy. Kenney sings along with the first verse, and I take the second. The drums have a tinny rattle at the very back edge, sprinkling bits of sound throughout. Then everything breaks for a deep cello swirl, which climbs into the rest of the music that starts to pick up again and lift the singer's voice. Kenney and I both sing along with the chorus as loudly as possible: shouting. Then all of the instruments stop and we're left with just the sound of hands clapping in the wake of the beat.

Kenney turns to me, beaming a smile. The kitten purring.

I laugh. "You know, dance class could be sort of fun. We'll see. I just don't want to have to wear any crappy outfits."

Kenney pulls into a parking spot at the community arts center, which is a square cinder block building with vertical slits for the energy-efficient windows that reflect the industrial resurgence in Greensboro during some of the '70s. She turns to me and touches her fingers to my forearm. "You won't have to wear any crappy outfits," she says with mock sincerity, in her imitation of my mother's voice.

When we get out of the car, Fred is waiting outside the building. He is perched beside the trash can that's next to the door. He looks like he is hiding.

"Hey, kitty cats," Fred says. It seems like he is always perching when he waits for us.

"Meow," Kenney says and rushes toward him. She flings an arm around him, pulls his head in toward her kiss on his cheek. Her boxy black, satin-covered purse bounces against his shoulder. I can't imagine that it isn't poking him, but he isn't annoyed.

*Tea Benduhn*

"So what's the deal here?" Fred asks. "Do we just go in? Are we supposed to wear leotards?"

"Just follow me." She leads us to a classroom tiled with odds and ends of mismatched earth-tone linoleum and puke-orange matted-down carpet in the entrance—the kind of floors like at school, only worse if that's at all possible.

There are five other people there. And all of them are older than my grandmother.

Florence and Gladys are wearing name tags and matching flowered green muumuus. They look like twins. Their hair is blue-white dandelion fluff, their perfume is definitely Church Lady Lilac. They are shapeless cream-puff women. Helen and Ike are another pair. Helen has on a periwinkle skirt suit and is rail thin, making me think her legs will crack like peanut brittle if she tries any sudden moves. But she also looks quite snappy with her silver and mother-of-pearl inlay horn-rimmed glasses attached to a librarian chain around her neck, and bright hot-pink lipsticked thin lips. While Helen's pretty short, her husband Ike is even shorter, hunched over with a bald head and strings of dyed black hair combed over his shiny skull. He wears a tan leisure suit.

Then there's a willowy woman with a helmet of flyaway wiry gray hair wearing a light purple leotard and maroon tights. She is stretching on a bar mounted along the mirrored wall.

"Hiiiiiiiii, Margaret," Kenney coos at the woman.

"Hello, dear." She smiles at Kenney.

"These are my friends Fred and Aurin," Kenney says.

"Welcome." Margaret smiles at us and straightens up, putting her foot back on the ground. "You can just put your things down in the corner, and join us in stretching."

Neither Fred nor I have "things" with us, so we just walk over to the group of senior citizens. Kenney loops her purse handles over a coat hook and kicks off her shoes. She jumps directly into the middle of the room, displacing a few wobbly-stepped individuals with her long stretches. She twists her waist and circles her arms like she's a windmill. Fred and I stand in the corner, and just look at each other. Fred shrugs, and I mirror him. Then we both sit down, take off our shoes, spread out our legs, and start reaching for our toes.

Kenney is still a windmill, and Fred and I face each other. We place the bottoms of our feet against one another's, then grab hands and alternately pull one forward, the other back, then switch.

"Ahem," Margaret says.

We stop and look up at her.

"We won't be needing to stretch quite that far today." She peers down at us with a stern look.

My cheeks flash hotness, and I can't look at anybody. I just look at the carpet along the wall behind Fred as I get up from the floor. I glance toward the door momentarily, and notice there is another person coming into the entrance.

Then I feel a jolt of electricity shoot through my fingertips as sweat covers the palms of my hands and coats my fingertips. I stiffen my head and try not to turn, not to look.

"Oh, hello," Margaret says.

It's Her. The Frisbee Girl. "Is this Ballroom Dancing?" she asks with that voice that scrapes shivers from the small of my back up my spine.

I look up at the ceiling and try to take in a breath. Then the whole class is hobbling around to see who Margaret is talking to, and I figure it'll be obvious if I don't turn with the rest of them. I concentrate on my facial muscles, try not to let them betray the thrill in my stomach.

"Come on in," Margaret says. "We're just about finished stretching, but you can put down your things and stretch a little more with us."

"Thanks." The girl smiles. Her cheeks round out with her smile. She's wearing a leopard print leotard with baggy black silky soccer shorts. She sits down and unties her black boots, taking them off to reveal striped tube socks. Her legs look strong, like she could break someone's neck with them.

"Okay, class, I think we're ready to begin," Margaret says.

Everyone faces her. They spread themselves into rows. Margaret tells us we're just going to start with the simple box step. We start with taking just one step, and practicing it several times. For some reason, even though it is simple, I cannot get this step right. And when we move toward two steps, my body is definitely not moving where she wants it to go. I keep using my left instead of my right, and going forward instead of backward. And forty-five minutes later, by the third, most complicated step, it is obvious that I am a disaster. Forget about doing a whole square. For some reason I want to skip the fourth corner and just make a triangle.

The twins are perfectly in step with each other. So are Helen and Ike. Fred is following tentatively, but doing it right. Kenney is almost as bad as me, but altogether so confident that it doesn't even matter. It seems as if she believes whatever moves she is doing are the right ones and that everyone else is wrong and screwing up when they aren't following her.

The leopard Frisbee Girl moves her body gracefully. While everyone else is bumping into one another and making a jumbled, clanking mess, Frisbee exacts the same fluid motions as Margaret.

And while I watch her, I'm thinking of the way a fountain pushes water effortlessly into the sky. And if she was in my movie, I would set her stretching against the background of an elaborate fountain of dancing water and the trickling sound of a rainmaker. She'd be wearing a green and blue bodysuit made to blend in with the winding river nearby.

And suddenly I have to pee.

So I find myself running to the bathroom. Then for some reason, by the time I get there I'm too nervous to pee. I must be in there forever, too, because before I even get a chance to go back to the classroom so I can stop screwing up and bumping into people, I can hear them going down the hallway. I can't believe class is already over, but it must have been a short session since it was the first one.

I rinse off my hands as quickly as possible, but by the time I open the door, she's already down the hallway and going outside. I don't even know what I would have said to her anyway.

Kenney and Fred are waiting for me near the classroom.

"Okay," I say. "I'm ready to sign up now."

"What?" Kenney's face screws up.

"Aren't we going to take the class?"

"I don't think so," she says.

"Oh come on, you know it was fun." Fred joins in my enthusiasm.

"That was terrible," Kenney says. "The both of you looked like fools."

"So?" Fred says.

By now I know I've got to take this class if it means that girl from the park might be here. Even if I *do* look foolish. "Oh come on, Kenney, you'll love it. Just think of how good we'll make you look in comparison."

We start walking out the front sliding glass doors. Kenney hangs on to my arm and kisses my cheek. "Okay, dearie. I guess if you really want to take dance class, I'll do it with you. Lord knows, I'd hate to be left out of your fun with Fred. The least we could do is come back next session and give it another try. Who knows? Maybe it'll get better." Then she pulls a brochure from her purse. "And I got this too, just in case. Fred thinks we should take pottery."

"I do not," Fred says. "I said poetry."

"Whatever," Kenney says. "Same thing."

Fred pirouettes to the car. Exit, stage left.

# *Fred's Fingers*

Here's where I would cut the camera to the next scene with a close-up shot on Fred's hands. His fingers are sturdy with short square nails. His hands look sure of themselves, not wimpy like they want to give up on his body. They look like they will do something, like they can make things happen. He has a scar on his left ring finger from where his Swiss Army knife slipped while he was peeling a mango last summer. The skin there is slightly discolored and purple-ish, somewhat vibrant against the pale white of the rest of his skin. There is a wispy tuft of black hair sprouting from each digit. Not too thick, not too thin. His hands are ghostly half of the time, and a dazzling display of statuesque alabaster elegance the other half.

He stands there, leaning against the monkey bars, pulling drags from his cigarette.

"You don't smoke," Kenney says.

"What do you call this?" Fred indicates the cigarette.

"Drama."

Fred ignores her comment, squints his smoldering coal eyes, and peers out to the field. He forgets for a moment that he's supposed to be smoking, and takes in a deep breath of real air, letting out a dog-sized sigh. Tony Simmons just knocked into Grant, the two of them tumbling to the grass. From the force of the fall, Tony rolls over Grant, pulling him along. Grant rolls on top of Tony and shoves off the ground like he's doing a push-up over Tony.

"Why don't you just talk to him?" Kenney asks.

Fred's eyes are glazed over. This happens from time to time. He just gets really sad about not being able to date anyone, when everyone else gets to. I try from time to time to remind him that I don't date anybody either, that it has nothing to do with *him* personally. It's high school: it just *is*. Of course, it doesn't help that I've never been interested in anybody before. Ever.

"What's he going to say?" I ask Kenney.

"What could be the worst that happens?" she asks, innocent.

Fred and I both glare at her.

Her eyes open wide, Marilyn Monroe. "What?" she asks, her voice small, surprised, soft. Of course she wouldn't understand. She has absolutely no clue what it's like to be perpetually single like us: me and Fred.

I missed it again.

Something must have happened in the field because here's Grant walking toward the tree line, by us. "No, screw *you*," he's shouting toward the field.

Grant is grumbling to himself as he walks toward us.

None of us speaks.

"Whoa." Grant looks up, startled that we're here. "Hey, man, you got a smoke?" Grant nods at Fred, guy-style. The secret code language they all have with one another that tends to manifest itself in head-nods at the mall.

"Yeah," Fred digs in his pocket.

"Got a light?" Grant asks.

Fred pulls out a plastic light-blue lighter, flicks the flint, sparks the flame, holds it up to Grant.

"Thanks, man," Grant says. "Did you see what they did?"

"Uh, no," Fred says.

Kenney, up to this point, and to her credit, has restrained herself from saying anything, this being Fred's moment. I suppose now she feels it's time to save us or something. "Who would *they* be?"

Grant looks over at Kenney, as if he hadn't seen that she was standing there. He curls up the side of his lip. "Like you weren't watching." Something in the way he says it makes Kenney look really small, makes my stomach churn a little.

Even Fred is a little taken aback by Grant's surliness. "What?" Fred standing up for Kenney. Fred sounding sarcastic and cocky. "You think the whole world is watching you all the time?"

"Sorry, man," Grant says. "Didn't mean to insult your lady." None of us bothers to correct him.

"My name's Grant, by the way." He holds out his hand for Fred to shake. "Thanks for the smoke." Grant's fingers are brittle and slender. They also look misplaced on his body, like they want to fly away from him. They're dirty, but small, petite, delicate. Up close, they make him look like a creature more than a god. Spindly and spidery, like an undernourished, disappointing rock star.

"Fred," Fred says, shaking Grant's hand, man-style. Like a preacher almost, so sturdy and sure. Fred betrays nothing of whatever may be somersaulting in his belly. He is so cool.

Grant nods at me, then keeps walking to the parking lot. Fred, Kenney, and I just stand there looking at one another.

Finally, Kenney says, "What a prick."

And Fred says, "Oh my god," and starts fanning himself.

And I let out a small nervous laugh.

"I just gave Grant Grayson a cigarette," Fred says. "I am never washing this hand again."

"Puh-leez," Kenney rolls her eyes. "Settle down there, Romeo."

"Did you see his stunning glory?" Fred asks.

"No. I just saw his mean, nasty self," Kenney says.

"That was not him," Fred says.

"Looked like him to me," I say.

"That's not what I mean," Fred says. "He was just upset about something. Oh *god*, that temper looks good on him."

"You're hopeless," Kenney says. "We have got to find a new object for your affections."

"No. What we need to do is find a way to get him alone again," Fred says.

"He thinks I'm your girlfriend." Kenney laughs. We all laugh.

Fred flicks off the built-up ash from his cigarette and stabs the butt into the edge of the merry-go-round platform. "So what's next?"

# Howdy, Pardn'r

**What's next is dance class.**

"Okay. Partners now," Margaret says.

What? Partners?

I don't have any idea who I'm going to dance with. The twins turn to each other, Ike to Helen. Fred grabs me, probably in order to evade Kenney, so Kenney and Frisbee Girl turn to one another. I place one hand on Fred's shoulder and hold the other.

"Decide who is Partner A and who is B," Margaret says.

I'm Partner A and Fred is B, or so I think, but when Margaret tells A to step forward and B back, we both step forward and knock against each other's knees. I reach down and grab my knee to rub the pain out. Then we get back in position, agree upon who is who, and try again. This time I start stepping forward, but Fred pushes into me to move backward.

I look over at Kenney and the Frisbee Girl. Kenney looks incredibly awkward compared to Frisbee. Frisbee is moving exactly the way Margaret says to. Kenney is lanky and her movements are jerky. Frisbee takes Kenney's hands into hers and stretches them upward, spraying out to the sides like a water fountain then down, and flowing back into the beginning position to dissipate the negative energy Kenney has stored up. She guides Kenney to shake out her arms and loosen up the muscles.

Fred and I clank against one another, his bony elbows jutting into my sides, his sharp edges poking into me.

"I can't do this." Fred drops my hands and steps back, away

from me. "Your breasts are getting in the way."

"Well, your nonbreasts get in mine," I say. "You're too pokey and sharp."

"No. You're too soft."

Frisbee drops Kenney's hands and turns toward us. I'm certain she's either going to make fun of us for stinking so badly, or yell at us for screwing everything up. Instead she says to Fred, "I'll dance with her." She indicates Kenney. "This girl isn't as soft."

Kenney's mouth drops open slightly, then she exaggeratedly places her hands on her hips. Her eyebrows dart inward a little.

Fred quickly leaps away from me and grabs Kenney's hands from her hips. He swirls her away.

Frisbee takes each of my hands in hers and says, "Hi. I'm Neila."

So thank god she finally has a name. Now I can tell her mine. "Aurin," I say.

"Nice to meet you, Aurin," Neila says.

She leans her body in closer to me than Fred's was. Her hip touches mine, and I flinch, jump back a bit. Only an inch, but it seems like a mile.

"Relax," Neila says. "I'm not going to bite." She smiles widely to reveal that slight gap between her two front teeth. "You need to touch your partner to follow her movements."

I drift back in toward her hip.

She places her hand on my waist, her fingers curling into the small of my back. Her hip rests against mine, our thighs touching. A small surge of nervous electricity shoots through my wrists into my hands.

Neila's eyes smile. They are hazel with flecks of gold. I can feel the muscle tense inside her leg, guiding my backward step with her forward one. The tautness of her arms leads me into a forward step with her backward one. A slight press of her palm into my waist motions our sweep to the side.

"Weren't you at the park the other day?" she asks.

I nod.

"I thought so," she smiles. Her hips press mine into another back step. My legs feel like liquid. I'm not even thinking about where to move them; they're just going where hers guide.

I notice I'm not saying anything, then say, "We hang out there sometimes—Kenney, Fred, and me."

Neila nods. "Cool." Her movements slide mine along.

My legs are beginning to feel warmer, and I realize that I need to pee *again.* I separate my hip from hers, then bump her knee against mine, and feel like I'm dancing with Fred again. "Sorry," I mutter. "I gotta pee."

Her eyes squint into slits, and she looks at me sideways, smiling with half of her mouth. "Okay," she says.

Margaret claps twice and says, "Okay, class."

The partners drop one another's hands and separate into singular entities. I want to run to the bathroom, but since Margaret's talking, I don't want to be rude. Besides, Neila stands so close to me that I could lean my shoulder against hers. I can feel heat radiating from her body, warming mine.

"That was great," Margaret says, enthusiastic. "All of you did such a good job that I'd like you all to give yourselves a big hand." She starts clapping.

Kenney is clapping her hands above her head loudly. Fred's hands are low, his clapping muffled and brief. The others are clapping politely as if at their grandchild's ballet recital. Neila's clap is neutral, though good-natured. I push my lip forward with my hand and start chewing. I still need to pee.

"Class meets every Tuesday and Thursday," Margaret says. "You can sign up at the front desk. If you can't sign up today, come back next week."

I squeeze my thighs together and bite my lip a little harder.

Kenney waves me toward her. "Let's get out of here."

"I'm going to the bathroom," I say. Then I run out into the hallway. In my desperation, I've forgotten exactly which way to turn, but I know I'll find it.

# Kittens of Pru Underwater

Maybe my movie will start with an underwater scene. Water that isn't exactly tropical because I don't want this to be a beach kind of thing, but definitely warm with beams of sunlight shooting through the murky stillness. A lake, perhaps.

I'll be wearing a gray business suit; a string of plastic pearls will float from my neck toward the surface. My face will be obscured by mossy hair. My limbs will be thrown askew, because I've just jumped in.

There will not be any sound.

"Aurin! Get out of the bathroom." My brother Shawn bangs on the door.

"In a minute," I say. I'd practically have to drown myself in the bathtub before they'd leave me alone.

"You may as well just give up, ugly," Shawn says. "Your face isn't gettin' any better, no matter how long you stay in there."

My face. It isn't *that* bad, though I suppose I can also see how it isn't that good either. Sort of neutral, I think. My nose is regular sized and regular shaped, maybe a little small. My hairline is slightly egg-shaped and a little low, but if I leave my bark-colored hair to frizz, it's barely noticeable. Plus, it isn't like I'm completely lacking a forehead or anything. Certainly not the Neanderthal monobrow Shawn has. I guess my jawline is a little square, but whose face is a perfect circle anyway? And my eyes are just plain dark brown.

The only really upsetting aspect of my appearance is that I

am definitely rounder than Kenney, so she always makes me feel short and fat by comparison, though it's mostly my breasts that are so huge.

"Hey!" Shawn shouts and bangs on the door again.

"What's your freakin' hurry?" I ask when I open the door.

"Band practice," he grunts as he shoves past me. Shawn's going to be a famous drummer when he grows up. Yeah, right.

"What's the big deal? You're gonna stink by the time you get home anyway."

"Screw you, twerp."

I love my family.

Meanwhile, my room, of course, is a mess and Prudence is going to freak when I tell her I'm going over to Kenney's tonight. I could always shape the piles in my room enough to make her think I'm making progress on my spring cleaning, which has now lasted into summer. We've been working with this same illusion for years. She must have caught on by now, but I think we both play dumb in order to placate one another.

After finding a pair of pants that not only fit on my expanding round ass, but don't look overly dorky or like I'm trying too hard to look cool, I head downstairs to catch Kenney's chariot.

"Where do you think you're going, young lady?" Prudence asks.

"Over to Kenney's."

"Did you clean your room?"

Always this same drill. "Go look," I say.

Prudence finishes fluffing the decorator pillows on the love seat, and heads upstairs. I can practically hear her face twitching into a half-grimace of approval as she utters an audible sigh and says, "Okay."

I head to the basement to escape her while I wait.

"Hey, Dad, what's up?" I say.

"Many things . . . many things." He's pulling on his beard with his arms crossed tightly against his chest, and pacing back and forth. "The ceiling which is also a floor, to which there is another ceiling and so on, until you get to the roof, after which there are tree branches. Perhaps a few birds, clouds, air molecules, particles of dust, which are actually in various stages of settlement, the sky, other planets, stars, and infinite space. But you knew that, didn't you?" My dad, the smart aleck. "Actually, though, I'm working on this new idea for voice-activated lights. Why don't you tell me what you think?"

Okay, here's the thing about Henry: I don't know what he does in this basement every day. There are a lot of electronics that lurk about in a variety of stages from completely disembow-eled to mostly put together. I think he's inventing stuff. But then again, he may not be. Meanwhile, there are also several open beer cans littered about the surfaces, which range from cold to lukewarm, full to empty. He leaves these about because he forgets whether or not he's opened one, and where he has put the last. It is unclear to me whether this is due to his intense concentration on the electronics, or because he has already opened and drunk so many beers.

"So you wake up in the middle of the night," Henry says, "and the light switch is across the room. What do you do? Or how about this? A burglar breaks in at night . . ."

"Dad, I hope you haven't done too much work on it yet because they already have those." I hate being the beastly one to break his heart.

Henry starts pulling on his mustache and making a snorting

sound. His pacing increases speed. "Maybe so, maybe so . . ." He nods and walks around the corner.

Kenney's horn honks outside.

"Well, I'm going to let you get back to your work," I say and head back up the stairs to catch Kenney's ride while leaving Henry to swim around his basement.

When we get to Kenney's, she sits on the floor in front of the TV cabinet, bottom doors swung open. This is what we do all summer, every summer. Hang out in Kenney's living room or kitchen or backyard, or drive anywhere sixteen-year-olds are allowed to go.

"What's this?" I ask. *"The Exotic Kittens of Pru?"* I'm reading the title upside down from a book on the coffee table.

She pulls her dad's video camera out from the cabinet, swings the doors shut. "What?"

"This book. Oh. Never mind." *The Exotic Kitchens of Peru,* it says. There are giant four-color photographs of richly hued kitchens with wild plants and hand-painted tiles.

"That's what you are," Kenney laughs then plops down next to me, sinking into the dusty rose–striped couch.

"What do you mean?"

"Duh, Aurin. *Kitty* cat. Your mom is *Pru.*"

"Yeah, yeah, I know that." I roll my eyes, try to hide the flutter inside my stomach. Exotic. Maybe someone else finally sees it. "But what makes me," I try to sound natural, but trip a little bit over the word, "exotic?"

"Don't get so worked up about it," Kenney flicks her hand, splashing invisible water on my face. "It's just a word."

"Yeah," I say. Just a word.

My mom claims that I get my coloring from her Greek grand-father. When I was little, my father laughed and told me my mother was seduced by Gypsies. She used to toss her head back, and shake her long blonde hair in a swaying snakey motion when she laughed at the things that my father said. Now Prudence's hair is short and beige and Henry has forgotten about the Gypsies.

"We should make a movie," I say, while Kenney turns the camera over in her hands.

"Are you kidding?" She gets up from the couch, sits back in front of the TV cabinet and opens the doors. "My dad would *kill* us." She pushes the camera back to the exact place she got it from.

"Right," I say. "I forgot." I watch the back of Kenney's head, how her curls bounce when she closes the doors. I can't believe she's never been teased for looking like Annie with her hair cut. I guess it's because she *doesn't.*

"Hey," Kenney props her head back against the TV cabinet. "What do you think about that Neila chick?"

I think of birds. I can't *help* but think of birds every time I hear that word, "chick." And then there are the birds swirling around in my head and my stomach and my hands. I hope they don't fly out of my throat and carry me away by my feet when I open my mouth to speak. I shrug. "I don't know. How come?" My voice squeaks at the end anyway. I sigh to cover it up, hoping she didn't notice my nervous rush.

"Fred and I were talking, and we think we should try to hang out with her some. She seems pretty cool. So ethnic-chic."

The birds turn into angry, protective red bees. "Like she'd be a good investment for our images?"

"Oh come on now." A smile sneaks onto Kenney's face. "You don't have to be so suspicious of me." She holds out her arms, runs her hands up and down along them for display, then pulls up the corners of her short sleeves. "See? I've got nothing up them."

I have to laugh. No matter how often I think she's a climber, I can't help but love Kenney. "Yeah, I know."

"We just think it might be more fun to start hanging out with some new people."

I don't know why, but I feel sort of threatened. "You two thinking of *replacing* anyone I know?"

Kenney looks at me, dead-serious. "Yes. Aurin, we've been trying to come up with a more palatable way of telling you this, but now that you've figured out my secret plan with Fred . . . I guess there's no better way of breaking the news. We're sorry, but we'll have to let you go."

"Ha ha," I say. "Very funny. So where is this Fred person you talk so much about, anyway? Is he your imaginary friend?"

"Ooooh, who's the joker now?" Kenney chides. "He has to clean the pool. He said he'd meet us at dance."

I look at my watch. "Well, then?"

"Okay, Grandma," Kenney uses her small, elderly voice. "I guess we better be gettin' on out of here then, mosey along 'n' whatnot." She shuffles her feet, knees bent, shoulders slumped forward. "Come on, schweetie." She links her arm through my elbow.

# Dance, Take Three

Fred tells us he's gotten his neighbors Martha and Thelma to join too. They are an elderly pair of spinsters who often times wear coordinated outfits, and who Fred believes to be "on his team," as he says. And when we get there, they are indeed there and all fired-up and ready to go. Thelma is in a hot pink jogging suit, while Martha opts for the subtler, more sophisticated mauve.

"Glad to see you ladies," Fred winks at them.

Martha and Thelma turn to one another and touch arms and wrists. They are mightily pleased with Fred.

And here's what happens in class: Neila doesn't show up. I know that I didn't imagine her, though, because Kenney leans over and asks Fred, "Where do you think she is?"

And what's more is this: I can't dance at all. My knees are jutting everywhere, and my feet twist out of their ankles. And I actually fall and stumble and trip people. Thank god, I don't trip anybody over the age of fifty. But that does mean that Fred and Kenney are targets in my Danger Zone.

Margaret shoots me a few scowling glances. Even though she teaches amateurs, she's probably not used to seeing people screw up this much. I have no idea why I can't learn a simple box step.

What's worse: I don't have a partner. No one will dance with me. Least of all Margaret. She tried a few times out of pity, but ended up claiming that she prefers to watch the class to make sure everyone else can get it.

So I'm totally left out in the cold. And I am hating it.

"That was so much fun!" Kenney says after class. "You were so right, Fred. Those old people are wonderful!"

"See? I don't know why you ever even considered doubting me," Fred says.

"I'm not going back there," I say.

"What?" Kenney and Fred in unison. "You have to," Kenney says. "You're the one who wanted to keep coming."

"I changed my mind."

"Don't be ridiculous," Kenney says.

"In her defense," Fred says, "she *does* suck."

"Thank you," I say.

"Besides, she doesn't have a partner," Fred says. "'Cause no one will dance with her."

"Thank you," I say again. "That'll be enough defense for me for now."

"Yeah, where do you think Neila is anyway?" Kenney asks. "We were supposed to see if she wanted to hang out with us after class."

"Must be too busy, or didn't like it or something," I shrug.

"Yeah," Kenney says. "Couldn't make it because she was actually too busy hanging out with Grant, I'll bet." She shoots a look over at Fred to gauge his reaction.

He predictably bristles. "Why would you say that?"

"I'm just teasing. I'm sure she won't take your man," Kenney says. "Why don't we go to the park?"

So we go to the park, and they aren't there. We walk all the way to the Frisbee field, and there's a group of people playing. In fact, it even looks like Grant and Neila's team, though it's sort of hard to tell since all those Birkenstocks flopping around look the same sometimes.

"See?" Kenney says. "I told you they were probably screwing."

"One," Fred says, "you did not tell me they were screwing. And two: they are not screwing."

"Well, anyway, as you can see, there is a field full of Frisbee players and there is no sign of either Grant or Neila. Additionally, there was no Neila at dance class. Now where do you suppose they could be?"

"Sick?" I offer. I hope.

As we walk back through the trees toward Kenney's distinctively pink '60s convertible, a blue VW Squareback peels through the gravel, speeding away from us.

There's a note stuffed under Kenney's wipers. Kenney grabs it and reads it.

"Here." She shoves the note at me. "It's for you."

"Why would there be a note for me on your car? Besides, how would anyone know I was here?"

"Aurin, honey," Fred says. "You're *always* either here with us, or at dance—with *us*." He cranes his head over my shoulder. "What's it say?"

*Ah-ren/ O-wren/ Or-in (sp?):*

*Couldn't make it to dance. See you at Grant's party*
*tomorrow night.*

*—Neila*

And there are directions to Grant's place.

"I don't get it," I say.

"Duh," Kenney says. "She's inviting us to Grant's party." She plucks the note from my hands. "That is so cool. I guess now we'll find out what's up between the two of them."

"Other than your imaginary scenario?" Fred asks.

"Maybe she's not inviting us," I say. "Maybe she just thinks we're coming. Grant doesn't even know we're alive."

"He does too," Fred says. "I gave him a cigarette."

"Why would she think we were already going unless we were invited?" Kenney says. "Anyway, either way, we *are* going."

Fred crosses his arms and looks at me. He nods in agreement.

# Party Dood

So here I find myself, leaning against a wall at Grant's party. I don't even have to imagine a movie scene for this part because even though it's my real life, it already looks exactly like one of those dumb high school ones with the obligatory party scene.

Over here we've got some kids with their hair dyed all sorts of colors, then some other kids nearby with shaggy hair sporting the retro look, and over there, some others looking very stylish and up-and-coming, all of them sprinkled amid the beer cans and cigarette butts. Complete with the requisite buzzing murmur of a crowd. They are all so fake. Fake. Fake.

And if the guests aren't enough to make me puke, Grant's living situation is. He's got his own apartment made out of the converted garage, which consists of a bedroom, living room, and bathroom. The garage apartment is connected to the main house by a hallway, and the party flows between Grant's place and his dad's. I think his dad is the president of some construction company or something. Or maybe a furniture guy.

"Dude, now *this* is *some* party," a guy's voice floats above the general din. He sloshes over to one of the shaggy guys and sloppily grazes his jacketed shoulders against several other people who look at him briefly, then return to their conversations. None of them seem to notice that it's strange for that guy to wear a jacket in the middle of summer.

Everyone looks animatedly bored.

I close one eye and squint the other while watching the guy with the jacket weave through the crowds. "You know what your problem is?" Kenney's voice drills into my ear. "You don't know how to mingle."

"Thank you so much for informing me of my problems, Kenney, because I was just thinking about how I couldn't quite figure out what was wrong with me," I say.

Kenney rolls her eyes exaggeratedly and laughs at me. "That's not what I mean. You know what I mean."

"But I don't know anybody," I say.

"What do you mean you don't know anybody? You know me and Fred."

"Big deal," I say. "I can talk to y'all any time. Besides, where is Fred anyway? Talking to those guys over there." I point at Fred, who is seriously turning on the charm. He's pulling his queeny bit, which he never does unless he's trying to make people laugh. And it works too, since they never know how to take him. Fred's motto is: *How can they make fun of me if I get to it first?*

Kenney rolls her eyes again then turns to some bleach-blond guy, tapping him on the shoulder and giggling about something. I cram myself farther into the corner, testing the flatness of the wall against my back. I go back to my role as wall-holder-upper.

From my incognito position, I watch Kenney's mouth open and close animatedly, peals of laughter periodically floating from her direction. The blond guy she's charming wears a smirk on his face. The thought-bubble above his head reads: *whoa, I can't believe this babe is actually talking to me. I'll try to act cool, not too interested, but enough to keep her hanging.* He must be a freshman.

Another guy, who looks like a catalog model, walks past them and Kenney brushes his sleeve with her fingertips. He joins their conversation. The first guy slightly inflates his chest, an attempt to display base machismo. Kenney giggles with both of them, and pushes on the catalog model's arm, sending him away. When his back is turned, Kenney turns closer to the blond guy and wrinkles her nose.

The blond guy grabs another guy's shoulder, and steers him over to their conversation. This guy is dramatically short. He has a bit of a mustache and I can tell from here that he is probably wearing terribly wrong shoes. The blond pats the short guy's chest. The gist of his action is: *this is my buddy from church camp. We go way back.* The short guy slimes closer to Kenney and she smiles, but her eyes do not shine. I recognize the smile of politeness and disdain. Blond has had enough of short guy, and pushes him in a friendly manner, back into the crowd. Short guy, being a pawn for Kenney and Blond's game, willingly goes, but not before turning back and looking up and down the length of Kenney. When his back is turned to them, she flicks her fingers after the short guy, as if shooing away some distasteful bug.

Having enough of the Kenney Bayliss show, I scan the crowd to see if there's anyone I want to talk to. Particularly, Neila. She isn't here yet, and I have a feeling she isn't coming. I'm beginning to think I was dragged along here for no other reason than as a support system for Kenney and Fred in case they accidentally end up with no one else to talk to. In case they run out of people to network.

"Here, girl, you need one of these," some guy says to me and thrusts a cheap-looking can of beer into my hand.

It's Grant.

"So, what brings you here?"

I shrug. Oh my god, Grant is talking to me. Fred is going to absolutely die when he sees this. "My friends, I guess," I say.

"Oh yeah, which ones are they?"

"That guy over there," I point to Fred. "And her." I touch Kenney's elbow, but she shrugs me off and turns her back further on me. She's standing in the middle of a group of boys and has her long arms draped over the shoulders of one of them, leans dangerously close to another one's lips. Then she giggles and presses her hips against someone else's side. Apparently she doesn't see me talking to Grant, and thinks that I'm just trying to get her attention for my own purposes.

"Some friends," Grant says. "I don't remember inviting them."

"You didn't," I say.

Then he shrugs and half-laughs, "'Course I don't remember inviting half of these people."

"Neila did," I say.

"She did?" He sounds surprised. "So my little cousin invited all these people?"

"Not all of them," I say. "Well, I don't know. Maybe she did. I just meant . . ." God, why do I keep stumbling over what I'm trying to say? What *am* I trying to say? *"Your little cousin?"*

"Yeah, I guess we don't look too much alike, huh?" He laughs.

"You mean, aside from being different colors?" I say. "You're both *cute.*" Real smooth, Aurin.

Then he's silent forever. I may as well just say: *gee, golly, Grant Grayson, you're just so gorgeous I don't even know how to act around you* and giggle a whole lot while twisting my hair around my fingers or something. But instead I just wish he would go away, or that I hadn't said that, or something.

"So, what school do you go to?" he asks.

"Yours," I say. Yay! Another point for me and my social coolness. Now he'll definitely know that I know who he is and that he doesn't know who I am. That shifts our footing some more, puts him considerably further into the way-cooler range, as if he weren't already. "I mean, you go to Shady Brook, right?" The Save.

"Yeah," he smiles. "I haven't seen you around."

"Oh," I say. Like I'm not in your cool little circle of friends, okay? So you wouldn't know of my existence anyway because I reside in Geeksville.

"Cool." He nods. What's up with that? Nothing I am saying is cool. This guy must be totally drunk.

"Duuuuude." Some guy half-tackles Grant. It's Tony. "This is the best party all summer, man."

"Hey, Tony, this is . . ." He stalls, realizing he doesn't know my name.

"Aurin," I say.

"Funky name," Grant says, pleased.

Tony nods, then gets distracted by someone else and heads off.

Grant turns and looks at me for kind of a long time. It's making me nervous. "Yup." I say and make a smack-pop sound with my lips.

"Weren't you at the park the other day?" he asks.

"Yeah."

"I thought I saw you before. You were with those other two, weren't you?"

I nod. "Kenney and Fred," I remind him of their names.

"That dude seemed pretty cool," Grant says.

"He is," I say.

"Someone said he's gay. Do you think it's true?" Grant asks. His tone surprises me, since it doesn't sound demeaning at all, but genuinely interested. I guess I just expect Grant to be homophobic, considering his performance at the park the other day.

I shake my head. "I don't *think* he is," I say. "I already *know* the answer." I'm not sure if Fred really wants me revealing this information to Grant. It probably isn't my place to say. Even though no one seems to harass Fred at school, you never know how people are going to act once they know the truth.

Grant shrugs. "Well, you know, it would be cool if he was." He says this like it really doesn't matter to him one way or the other. As if he was just making light conversation and nothing really makes a difference in the big scheme of things.

Or, I could just be projecting. "So listen," Grant says. "I'll see you around, okay?"

"Later," I say. Finally. Thank god, he's going.

"Hey," he says, like an afterthought. "Can I get your number, you know, just in case?"

"I'll be around," I say. "Believe me." I roll my eyes. "I'm at the park *all* the time."

He nods. And then, finally, he goes.

I look around for Kenney and Fred, but can't see them. They must be obscured by all the smoke, or in another room. And I still haven't seen Neila. I want to leave.

"This is boring," some girl near me complains, and grabs the hand of the guy next to her.

Fast-forward through a few more interactions, and the room is starting to empty. I guess people are starting to find places to make out, so I go outside to look for Kenney and Fred.

I haven't even left the wraparound porch of his dad's house before I hear someone say, "Hey, girl," to me. I guess people must not have names around here, just genders. But it's that voice, the one that rides the edge of sugar and gravel. My elbow gets warm and tingly where it's touched. I turn around.

I can feel my face involuntarily leap into a smile when I see Neila.

"Where you been?" she asks. "I been lookin' for ya."

"You have?" I say before I can think of a less dorky way to react. My throat closes slightly, causing a halt in my voice.

"You leaving?" she asks.

"Yeah," I say. "I was just looking for my friends."

"You can't go yet," she says. "I haven't even had a chance to talk to you." She places her hand on my elbow so lightly, so naturally, and guides me to a corner of the porch, out of the way of the door. We lean up against the house. "I at least wanted to find out a little more about you. We never get a chance to talk. The more we bump into each other without speaking, the more mysterious you become."

"Go for it," I say, then feel my cheeks instantly turn boiled lobster red. "I mean, what would you like to know?"

She shrugs. "I dunno. I don't even know how to spell your name. Or what your favorite color is. Or what kind of movies you like. Anything. Tell me anything."

"That leaves such an open space," I say. "Like some sort of frightening essay with nothing but a blank page. Okay. My name." I tell her how it's spelled, then I try to think of a favorite color, but they all come rushing in. The yellow of her hair, the smooth light brown of her skin, the sparkling topaz of her eyes, the jealous green of Kenney's—"Oh crud! Kenney." But why would Kenney be jealous? What of? Me having a friend other than her, or her not getting to know the newest cool girl first?

"I'm sure she's fine," Neila says. "Tell me more." She tilts her head to one side. "Tell me a secret."

Instantly a block goes up. I don't have any secrets, at least not any that I can think of to share. But then, because she says it like we're in fourth grade, I start to think of one.

"I never tell any of my friends about this," I say, "but I want to make a movie about my life."

"Why don't you ever tell them?" she asks.

I shrug my shoulders. "I dunno. They'll think it's stupid."

"Why would they think that? What'll it be like?"

"I don't even know yet. I don't have anything for it to be *about*. Just scenes. And all of those scenes will have to lead up to something, but I don't know what."

She doesn't say anything, but keeps looking at me, and now I'm starting to feel stupid, and embarrassed for sharing. But I couldn't think of anything else. I don't have any other secrets. At least I don't think so.

Then she says, "I'm sure there will be *some*thing."

I'm feeling less embarrassed now.

"Just try not to think so hard about it, and I'm sure something will come up."

"What about you?" I ask. "What is your secret?"

Before she can tell me, Kenney and Fred are climbing up the porch steps, looking scowly with their knees jutting up at extreme angles.

"Where have you been?" Kenney asks in this really motherly tone. I almost expect her to say "young lady" along with it.

"First I was talking to Grant . . ." I say.

"Really?" Fred perks up.

"Yeah, right," Kenney says. "Can we get out of here now, or what?"

I want to ask if her antagonism has anything to do with the noticeably absent blond guy, but I'd rather not get snapped at.

I shrug. "I guess so."

"Can I catch a ride?" Neila asks.

I look at Kenney, who is standing with one hand on her hip, car keys in the other. Fred is standing like a slouched block, ready to be molded anywhere you put him. Kenney sighs with a slightly visible eye roll. "Where do you live?"

"Not too far. But if it's a problem, I can find another way. Or I can just crash here and have Grant take me in the morning." An instant picture of her shiny smooth knee pointed toward the sky, some drunk guy from the party tangled around her, flashes to my mind. I don't want to leave Neila here.

And luckily Kenney says, "Hop in."

When we get to Neila's house, she offhandedly says, "We should hang sometime," but doesn't allude to us finishing our conversation. She says it like one of those polite things you're supposed to say to people you met at a party that gave you a ride home, not at all like we could have possibly been sharing a bonding moment back there on Grant's porch. And I can feel a jump in the attention of everyone in the car—dogs leaping for a bone, so to speak. Or cats for a fish.

"See you Tuesday," Kenney says as Neila closes the car door.

Neila doesn't say anything in return, and I watch her legs kick through the headlights, breaking the beams that flash on her, and reform when she's gone. Even in the shadows of her doorway my eyes can trace the curve of her calves.

# Sleeping Beauty

**The morning sun breaks through my concentration** on sleep, but Kenney seems not even the slightest bit fazed by the event. While I rest on the fold-out foam chair/bed that she keeps in her room for me, she lies like a princess, basking in the light that shines on her fluffy white lace-covered bed. I half expect cartoon birds to come chirping in and start tying ribbons into bows.

In my movie, some beautiful people wake up next to one another. One brings the other breakfast. They lounge around on fluffy pillows and cuddle in the morning sunlight. They are in bliss in one another's presence. They bask in the "morning after" glow.

In real life, I'm alone on the floor and Kenney's alone in her bed.

Last night she brushed those wrists across more than one neck. She's like that, I guess, indiscriminate about who she touches. I don't know what makes her so free to touch everyone when I'm so afraid of it. I wonder what it would take for me to shake off my inhibition and elevate myself to her princess status.

I want to poke her in the ribs.

But I know that will incur the wrath of the beast. Not that Kenney's a beast exactly, but sometimes she can be pretty foul in the morning.

Her shoulders tense and rise as she props herself up on her elbows, then palms, stretching like a cat. She rubs her eyes and yawns, twists around, then sits up.

"Good morning, sweet pea!" Not foul today though, I see. She leaps down from her ivory tower and lands on my sleeping bag, with a knee positioned on either side of me. "Ugh, you smell like a bar." She backs away and covers her nose.

"Well, no duh, you don't smell much better," I say. "We were surrounded by beer and cigarettes last night, what do you expect?" I shove her away so I can sit up.

"We better get rid of that before I take you home," she says. "Prudence will kill you—she'll be able to smell you a mile away. Your immaculate-scented home will screech 'invader' to her as soon as you step foot near it. Here." She grabs a towel that's hanging over her closet door and hands it to me. "Go take a shower and give me your clothes. I'll run them through the dryer with a fabric softener sheet."

"Thank you, big sister," I say, taking the towel and walking into her gigantic closet that's practically the size of another room. I take one of her robes and wrap it around myself, hand over my clothes, then head toward the downstairs bathroom, where I always shower when I'm over at her place. Luckily there are enough bathrooms in her house that we can both shower at the same time, and eliminate the uncomfortable wait of being in another person's house without anything to do while waiting for them to finish. The trick is to avoid running into her family, since I always feel the need to say hello or be polite, and they never talk. Amend that: her brother Aubrey and father Earl don't talk, they mumble. Her mother usually asks if we plan to go swimming. We never swim.

I tiptoe down the stairs from Kenney's attic room through the dusky, windowless hallway. At the bottom of the stairs I pause and listen. There is no sound of movement, but that doesn't mean anything, since her family is rather sedentary as well as muted. I slowly round the corner and look for shadowy motion. Nothing. I look out the front door and see only Kenney's car. Then I remember it's Sunday; they're all at church.

After showering in the brown-tiled, mucky soap-scum slimed, hair clump-cornered bathroom, I find my mostly fresh-smelling clothes lumped in a pile on top of the toilet seat. I'm so glad to have a friend like Kenney who will save my ass like that. I really love her sometimes.

Dressed, I follow cabinet-door thumping sounds into the kitchen. "Hey, hunny-hunny," Kenney says when I emerge.

"What are you doing?" I ask. All of the cabinet doors are open, and Kenney is peering into the refrigerator.

"I was just wondering, if you put coffee through a Britta, would you have caffeinated water?" she asks.

"Why do we want caffeinated water?"

"I dunno. To make stuff."

"Couldn't we just drink coffee?"

"Yeah, but that's not as fun." She closes the refrigerator door and sighs. "There's nothing to eat. Let's go out. We can get Fred too, if he's awake yet. It *is* only nine, after all."

"Crud. Kenney, I've got to get home. If Prudence doesn't kill me for smelling like a bar, she'll definitely kill me for being late."

"What, do you have plans today?"

"We're supposed to have a family barbecue, so I have to help Pru run some errands. And then she wanted to take me to the mall for some school stuff."

"School doesn't start for another month and a half. Besides, you hate the mall."

"I know. It was her idea, not mine. She thought it would be a good mother-daughter thing to do, and she's an early riser, so I just know she's been waiting for me since the crack of dawn."

"Hey, you know who works at the mall?" Kenney slips herself up onto the counter, not exactly the position of someone who is getting ready to take me home.

"No."

"Grant Grayson."

"Oh great."

"We can get Fred and all go together. Then we can come over for the cookout. It'll be fun."

"Um, Kenney, no."

"Why don't you just get Prudence to give you her credit card and we'll go without her?"

I roll my eyes. Kenney never gets this. "It doesn't work like that in our house. First of all, Prudence doesn't have a credit card. Second of all, if she's scheduled something for us to do together, I should follow through with my end of the bargain because at least she's trying to be nice, and not nagging me about being so lazy. I actually *want* to get along with my family. It makes life easier."

"All right, miss grumpity grump," Kenney slides off the counter. "I'll take you home."

"Thank you."

"But can I still come to the cookout?"

"No."

"Why not?"

"It's a family thing."

"And you don't consider me part of the family?" She links her arm through my elbow and leans on my shoulder.

I don't say anything.

"Well, thanks a lot," she says.

Kenney's copper eyebrows close in on themselves as she wrinkles her disappointed forehead. She grabs a set of keys from the wicker basket next to the microwave. She clomps her brown clunky untied shoes up the stairway to get her purse. When she comes back, her shoes are tied, and her chin is carefully positioned into the mask of stillness. She's trying to smooth away annoyance, but the crinkled skin around her eyes won't let her get away with it. Every facial muscle is taut.

"You can still hang out with Fred today, and make caffeinated water without me," I say as we get into her car.

"That's not the point. You're ruining my fun," Kenney says.

"There's always more fun to be had," I say. "Besides, I'm not going to be a whole lot of fun with you mad at me anyway."

Her head is purposefully positioned forward, her eyes focused on the road. The corner of her mouth twitches up a little bit. Her cheeks begin to loosen. Her frozen face begins to melt while her shoulders relax and she becomes normal again. "Okay, you're right," she laughs. "Besides, who wants to hang out with you and Pru anyway?"

"Exactly my point," I say.

"Anyway, oh my god, I can't believe we were at a Grant Grayson party last night," Kenney says. "That is *so* cool of us."

"I remember," I say. "I was there."

"You were?" Kenney says with mock surprise while she raises her eyebrows into perfect bridgelike arcs. "I barely even noticed, since you left the room after the first half hour."

"No I didn't."

"Whatever. Where did you go anyway?"

"Grant led me to a secret room in his dad's house," I say.

"Bullshit," Kenney says.

"Okay, no. I was just talking to some people. So did you have fun?" I don't know why I ask her this, since she's going to tell me she had the best time whether she did or not. She's got to keep up appearances, even with me.

"Are you kidding? Of course I did. There were all these cute guys . . ." and blah blah blah. She retells me basically everything I saw, and leaves out most of the parts that don't appeal to her, like the part where the blond guy wasn't there anymore by the end of the party and the part where she didn't get his number, and probably the part where his girlfriend showed up.

We pull up to my house. "Well, chicky-poo, have fun at your family thing and call me later!" Kenney kisses her fingers and waves little-kid style at me as I hop out of her car. Boy, is she ever in a few moods today.

# There's No Place Like Home, Click, Click, Click

Walking up the steps, I can tell our living room windows are open because I hear my parents arguing all the way out here.

"Prudence, that is not what I said." Henry's voice is calm and pushing down on the thickened, dense air.

"Yes, it is. You think I'm being irrational." Pru's voice is jagged.

Great. And Kenney wonders why I don't invite her to my little family functions?

I shove my key into the lock and push open the door. "Hi, guys," I say and quickly walk past them to the stairs.

"Just a minute," Prudence says after me, but I pretend I don't hear, and keep walking up to my room. I toss my bag onto the bed and notice what a mess Kenney and I left my room yesterday, then wade through to the bathroom, which connects Shawn's room to mine—Brady Bunch style.

As usual, the door is pulled shut and locked because Shawn forgets that his little sister is supposed to be sharing his kingdom.

So I have to go around to his side, through his room, which is dark and gray and covered with boy stuff—jeans, a guitar case, sock balls, empty matchbooks, posters, an open box of condoms that he probably never really gets a chance to use. I hold my breath and tiptoe through as quickly as possible, as if I'm in some sort of sanctuary. His side of the bathroom door is closed as well. Figures.

I push on the door, but it won't open. The resistance seems to be coming from something large, heavy, and soft-ish pressed directly against the door. I push again, harder, expecting to move whatever is blocking my entrance. A noise comes from the other side of the door. "Wha—?" —a drowsy, confused, scratchy version of Shawn's voice.

"Shawn, what are you doing?"

"Huh?"

"Are you sleeping in the bathroom?"

"What?" Shawn sounds annoyed now.

I am able to push the door open a little farther. Shawn is curled into a semifetal position, wedged between the toilet and bathtub. "Get up," I say.

Shawn starts huffing a lazy laugh. "Dude, I guess I passed out," he says as he gets up and stumbles past me to crash on his bed.

Lovely.

But at least with my brother out of the way, I can now change for my performance with Pru. I put on my favorite everyday summer dress. It's knee-length and made of breathable cotton with an orange-and-red-on-dark-blue floral pattern that looks like some kid drew it. I go back downstairs where Prudence is pouring sugar into freshly brewed tea. Henry is pacing back and forth from the kitchen to the living room, his arms crossed, chewing on his mustache.

"Do you know what time it is?" Prudence asks, her voice a little softer than it was when I came in a few minutes ago.

"I dunno. A little after nine, I guess."

"Ten fifteen."

"Wow! Time goes pretty fast, huh?"

"And you are late."

We stand there looking at one another for a moment.

Henry is still pacing. He opens his mouth, about to say something, then doesn't.

In that movie where I'm in the water, my mother is the shark and Henry is a minnow. Shawn is the good-looking surfer guy. Prudence leaves Shawn alone because he is too big and slippery and there's nothing that can be done with him. But she swallows Henry in one full gulp. There Henry lives, swimming around in her shark stomach.

In real life, my dad goes down to his basement.

I break a smile at my mom. "So what's on our strict agenda for the day?"

It's the word "agenda." She knows I'm making fun of her, so she softens a little bit and says, "Aren't we going to the mall?" The corners of her eyes crinkle when she smiles.

# Pru's Retail Therapy

Since the entire car ride is all about Prudence mwah-mwahing about her boss, the architect, I'll fast-forward to this conversation:

We're walking past the music store. "So, sweetie, did you and Kenney have fun last night?"

"Sure."

"Well, what did you girls do?"

I shrug. "The usual. We went out to get something to eat, went to the park, hung out with Fred some."

"You know, I think that Fred might like you."

"Mom, *please.*" She is so clueless. "Kenney and I have been friends with Fred since he moved here. Of *course* he likes me; he's my *friend.* Besides, in case you forgot, he's *gay.*"

"You know, honey, things change when you get older." She obviously can't hear certain things. "Sometimes people develop feelings . . ."

I am going to be sick.

"Oh! Look over there." Prudence points at exactly the kind of store I never want to go into, *Tripping Days-E.* The sign has big yellow letters that look hand-painted, but are clearly some version of a '90s font made to look '60s. Plastic beaded curtains line the entranceway, but they are tied to the sides of the opening to prevent lawsuits from some suburban mom's kid walking into the curtain and poking out an eye or something.

Prudence steers ahead. "Let's go in there. Come on, it'll be

"Likewise. I don't think Aurin has mentioned you to us before."

"Well, we just met," Neila says.

"Oh, isn't that nice?" Prudence says. To me, she says, "I thought you were out with Kenney and Fred all weekend."

"I was," I say.

"Oh, well, actually, we met a little before that," Neila says. "In dance class."

Prudence arches an eyebrow. "Dance? Aurin, wouldn't you like to invite your new friend over for our barbecue this afternoon? Neila, do you like zucchini?"

"You don't have to," I say.

"I'd love to." Neila smiles.

# Eggplant

"Hi, is this where Aurin lives?" I can hear Neila's voice at the front door.

"Yeah. Who are you?" Shawn asks.

"Neila. Who are you?" she returns.

I run down the stairs. "Hey, Neila, glad you could make it. Did you find the house okay?"

"I'm here, aren't I?" she smiles.

"This is my brother Shawn," I say.

Neila nods. "We met."

"Oh, Neila, so glad you could make it." Prudence comes in, polishing a spoon. "We were just setting the table. Aurin, why don't you get Neila something to drink? What would you like, dear?"

Neila shrugs. "What do you have?"

"Come in the kitchen, I'll show you the choices," I say. My toe catches on the carpet as if I've never walked with these feet on this space of floor before. I stumble and continue walking. Neila trips on the doorway between the living room and kitchen, where carpet becomes tile.

"Pretty rough terrain in here," she giggles. I can't believe she's giggling. I feel like an idiot, but am slightly relieved to think that she's either as self-conscious as I am right now, or pretending to be clumsy to make me feel better.

I laugh with her, then open the refrigerator door. I can feel her stare on the back of my neck as I call out, "Orange juice, tea, water, milk, Coke."

"Water," Neila says. Standard guest request.

"Big glass or small?" I turn around, holding the water pitcher and closing the refrigerator door.

"You didn't want me to come, did you?" she asks without even a trace of a smile.

The pitcher gets heavy, so I set it on the counter and begin nervously opening, closing, and opening the cabinet doors again. I pull out two glasses and place them on the counter. Neither of us speaks while I do this. Instead of answering her question, I ask, "Um, is one of these okay?"

She looks confused by my response and says, "Did you hear me?"

Maybe she thinks I have a hearing problem, which I sort of do at this point because I can feel all of the blood from my body rushing loudly into my brain, and clouding out other noises.

Neila steps toward me. Her body is incredibly close to mine, and I almost think she's going to touch me. Her cheek brushes past mine and I can smell the patchouli lingering in her hair from the store where she works. I wonder when she'll tell me her secret from the party, but am too nervous to ask. She reaches out and takes one of the glasses from the counter. I scoot out of the space between Neila and the counter, and bump my elbow into the refrigerator door handle.

"Ow!" I flinch and grab my elbow, which causes my arm to slap Neila lightly on the shoulder. She has already moved into the space I was occupying, which makes me wonder if I hadn't moved, where would she be? She's pouring water into her glass, and some of it spills out when I knock into her. "Sorry," I say. I am still holding my elbow.

"Are you okay?" she asks.

"Yeah, yeah. Just clumsy," I say.

"Girls!" Prudence calls from the back porch. "Supper's ready."

Neila is looking into my eyes, searching for something. Her face is so poised that her hair is the most animated part, springing from her head like it's alive.

I want to grab one of the curls and feel it bounce between my fingers.

She takes in a quick short breath like she's going to say something.

"I guess we should go eat," I say. Then we head out to the back porch.

"There you are," Prudence says. "Oh, Neila, is that all you're drinking? We've got Coke."

"I don't really like Coke, Mrs. . . . ?" Her voice falters at the end, as if she's questioning what to call my mother.

"You can call me Prudence. This is Henry. And you've met Shawn?"

Neila nods.

My dad is standing at the grill. He says, "Mr. and Mrs. Jondiss are my parents." He laughs at his own joke.

Prudence ignores him. "Now, what is it with you girls not liking Coke? That's all Shawn will drink."

"It's the bubbles," Neila and I both say.

Neila lifts her eyebrows. "It's too scratchy," she says.

"Well, I hope you like eggplant, we've got plenty of it."

"Eggplant?" Neila's voice squeaks.

"Henry grilled some summer squash, too."

Neila nods.

Prudence starts grabbing plates and dishing out the grilled

vegetables. She's practically flinging the plates like Frisbees into our hands.

"I'm not eating this crap," Shawn says. He leans back in his chair and pushes away his plate. "I don't eat purple food." I can't believe he is my *older* brother—the one who thinks he's so much cooler than me. "Where are the burgers? Who ever heard of a barbecue without any real food?"

"You knew we were trying something new today," Prudence says. "Your father spent all afternoon preparing this meal, I'd at least like you to try it."

I cannot even look at Neila.

"You are embarrassing your sister," Prudence says.

Henry stands at the grill, tongs in hand. His face does not reveal much behind his beard, but then he places the tongs onto the platter, crosses one elbow up onto the other hand, and starts pulling on his mustache to chew.

"Should I go?" Neila quietly asks me, so that only I can hear. I shake my head.

Shawn pushes himself away from the table and knocks over his chair in a great display of maturity. "I'm going to get some real food," he yells as his footsteps stomp through the living room. He returns with a box of sugar-coated cereal. He is *so* generic.

"So, Neila, where are you from?" Prudence smiles politely.

Shawn leans back, digging his arm deeply into the cereal box, rustling the flakes and rattling the package as loudly as possible. He tosses a handful at his face and crunches loudly. With his mouth full he says, "Ma, why do you always gotta think someone's not from here just because she's black?"

Oh great, Neila's just going to be begging for my friendship now.

"That isn't what I meant," Prudence says. "Why are you being so sensitive? I was only making conversation." She turns her head back toward Neila and plastifies her smile.

"I'm from here," Neila says. "My parents went to college here."

"Isn't that nice?" Prudence says. "Henry almost went to college." Pru darts a dagger glance at my father, who starts pacing across the deck and around the grill.

Neila clears her throat. "Good eggplant."

Henry is still pacing, but realizes it's probably time to start speaking. He slows down and drops his hands to pick up his opened can of beer. "Thanks. I marinated it in olive oil and balsamic vinegar with a sprinkle of rosemary and garlic. The squash has a little bit of cracked pepper and lemon juice."

"Delicious," Neila says.

We all begin eating and everyone is quiet. Prudence shifts in her seat, deciding whether or not she should start talking again. I know she wants to, because the silence is thick and heavy and awkward. She opens her mouth a few times and closes it back. Finally, she decides she cannot bear the silence any longer. "So how do you girls know one another?"

I roll my eyes. "Haven't we gone over this already?"

"Okay. So, Neila, what do you like to do in your spare time?" Prudence asks.

Neila brings her hand up to her throat and pinches her thumb and forefinger along the edge of her jawline, starting at the back and smoothing her grip forward to her chin. Then she makes a muffled clicking sound with her tongue. Prudence wrinkles her forehead, trying to decide if she's supposed to be deciphering some sort of code. Neila strokes her throat lightly with the tips of her fingers. She takes a drink and swishes the water around in her mouth. Then she swallows and starts scratching at her face around her mouth. Her lips are getting pinker.

Everyone is staring at her. We all sit perfectly still, as if someone has pressed the *pause* button. Then they all break into motion—Henry grabbing his beer, Shawn crunching his cereal louder, and Prudence leaning forward and asking, "Are you okay, dear?"

Neila nods. "Sorry, I think I might be allergic to eggplant."

"You're allergic to eggplant?" Prudence asks. "Why didn't you tell us? Why did you eat it?"

"It only happens sometimes," she says.

"Can we get you anything?" I ask.

Neila shakes her head and brushes her throat with her fingertips again.

"Henry, why don't you get her a glass of water?" Prudence orders.

"She already has one," I say.

Neila smiles. "No, really, I'm fine." Her lips are getting a little puffy now.

"Benadryl?" Prudence hops out of her chair.

"I hope your throat doesn't close up or anything," I say.

"No, really, it's cool," Neila says. "It'll probably go away in a few minutes. It can't get too bad." She drops her hands from her neck and picks up her fork to take a bite of salad. She is so calm. "Thanks for dinner. It really is great."

"Heh-heh," Henry snorts through his mustache. "We don't usually try to poison our guests." His sense of humor. "What else are you allergic to? Maybe I can cook that next time."

Neila clicks her throat and smiles.

Next time. There won't be a next time. Neila will never speak to me again. This whole scene is too freakin' weird. My stomach ties itself into knots, looping around and around, threading itself in and out, making an intricate mess. Maybe it's trying to weave a tapestry in there. I'm done eating. No one else is touching their food.

Neila's knee bumps up against mine. She looks at me and smiles slyly, then turns her head away and her eyes down. She pulls up her lips inside her mouth, scratching them alternately with her teeth. "Maybe I could use a little Benadryl," she says shyly to her plate.

"Okay," I jump up.

Neila slides her chair out and stands up slowly. "Thank you again for the dinner."

"No problem." Henry is still chewing on his mustache and snorting his laugh. "Any time, kidd-o, any time." As we head toward my room, I can hear him muttering to himself, "Nightshade vegetables."

"So, this is your room." Neila nods her head as she looks around. While I go to the bathroom cabinet, she sits on my bed, running her fingers up and down her throat and making a piglike noise.

She lets out a loud laugh. "Sorry. It really itches. I shouldn't mess with it so much."

I open the medicine cabinet and shuffle through it. "Okay, well, I'm going to save your life in just a moment."

"Oh wow," I can hear her saying from my room. "I have this same vase."

I poke my head out and look, even though I know exactly

which one she is talking about because I have only one vase in my room. It's the ugliest vase on the planet: dark pink glass bubbles that show through milky white glass, shaped like a genie bottle with a huge, messy lip that looks like there was too much glass left over and the glassblower just decided to shape it into a scalloped flower-approximation. A family heirloom.

"You do not." My voice rises in mock disbelief.

She nods, puts the vase back down. "Picked it up at a thrift store." She takes the Benadryl I offer. "You know, I really like your family," she says. She drinks from our toothpaste-splattered bathroom cup to wash down the pill.

"You have *got* to be kidding," I say.

"They're entertaining," she says. "My family is *super* boring." She presses her fingertips into the soft part of her neck, right beneath the chin, then strokes down toward the pit between her collarbones.

I realize I'm probably supposed to say something.

"Well," she says, "I better get going. My parents are expecting me to be home soon."

I don't know why, but I extend my hand to hers. She takes it, and I pull her toward the door. Even when we're in the hallway, our hands are still touching. I can feel my palms beginning to sweat, so I let go and walk a little faster for a moment. When we get to the door, I still can't think of what to say, and my cheeks are burning.

"I brought you something," Neila says.

"You did?"

"You have to close your eyes," she says. My stomach does a little leap as I close my eyes.

She takes my hand and opens up my palm. Then she places

something warm and smooth, not exactly round, and a little bit heavy into my hand, then closes up my fingers around the shapeless object.

"Now open them."

And I do, and I look, and it's a rock. A beautiful brown-and-brown-and-brown striped rock. A parfait of chocolate and cinnamon and caramel.

"I thought of it when I saw you at the store," she says. "We have bunches of rocks, but this one I think matches you. It looks sort of like tiger's eye."

She hops from my porch stoop and heads toward her car. My heart is beating fast, and my ears and my eyes follow her. I realize I forgot to ask her about the secret, but something in the air has changed a little bit. Maybe I'll know what it is when I see her again.

# The Green Green Grass

"You did *what?*" Kenney is narrowing her eyes at me.

"HadNeilaOverForDinner," I mumble into my shirt.

"How could you do that to me?" Kenney's eyes are wide and offended, and maybe a little hurt. "Oh sure, you won't invite your *best* friend, but it's perfectly fine to invite over a *complete stranger.*"

"She's not a complete stranger," I say.

So, yes. Here we are again, hanging out in the park, only this time we're sitting in a patch of grass near the lake. And as anyone might have guessed, Kenney is threatening to disown me because I didn't have the decency to consider her while my mother was coordinating my social life. Not that I minded this time.

"I think it was a good idea," Fred says.

Kenney turns her glare on Fred.

"Well, you're the one who said we should start hanging out with her," Fred says. "Besides, Aurin, did you get any dish on her and Grant?"

"I found out Grant is her cousin."

"Is that all?" Kenney asks. "And how much time did you spend with her, not even bothering to call your best friend?"

"Kenney, I didn't mean to. It's just that Prudence invited her before I even knew what was happening."

"Aurin, that is absurd. You told me that very same morning it was a *family* event."

"Well, it was. Or so I thought."

This scene would be like a John Waters film with the crazy overcontrolling best friend who acts like a mother. A lot of saturated, cartoony colors. "Kenney, look. I'm sorry, but what else do you want me to say? You know how my mother is. And besides, like I told you, it was a disaster. My family is a bunch of freaks." Cut to still shot of old-timey circus freak show with the faded pastel and black glitter aesthetic. Henry is the cowardly man in a lion's suit, Shawn the sad clown, and Prudence the boa-constrictor lady.

"Well, that's true," Kenney says.

"And there *was* the embarrassing allergic reaction," Fred reminds us. "But you *did* have a little fun anyway?" he asks hopefully.

I can't help but get that sunny yellow feeling again, the one that happens in my stomach and my knees and makes me smile. "Yes," I say. "I had fun anyway."

"So what's she like?" Kenney asks.

At the risk of offending her, I say, "She's great. She was really sweet and so nice to my parents and she liked them besides."

"I think someone has a cr-uu-uh-sh," Fred sings.

"Shut up," I say, and slap him lightly on the shoulder. "I do not." *Do I?* But I can't stop the smile. That must be what it is, since I must be beaming from ear to ear. Then again, maybe I'm just excited to have a new friend. She *is* fun, after all.

"Oh sure," Kenney says. "The two of you will practically fall in love with anybody." She's so absorbed in her own drama, she doesn't even realize what she might be saying.

"We do not," Fred says.

Kenney throws out her arms and stretches them as far and wide to the sides as she can, displaying her wingspan, and throws back her head while she wails, "But what about *meeeee?*" as dramatically as she can.

"I think its time for you," Fred tells her, "to get over it."

"I can't help it," Kenney says. "My friends are dropping like flies. First I lose you to Grant Grayson, and now her." Kenney points at me.

I decide to run with the melodrama she's created. "Maybe they've got another cousin," I shrug.

"What about that blond guy?" Fred asks. "Whatever happened to him?"

"Oh, *him*," Kenney says. "He was a dud."

Fred's attention shifts toward the Frisbee field, which is between where we are now and where we usually are on the playground. "Don't you mean stud?" Fred asks absentmindedly.

"Fred!" Kenney exasperatedly stomps her hands and feet on the ground and says, "Pay attention to me."

"So needy today," Fred says.

"I just want someone to love me," she whimpers and pouts. And the winner for most dramatic actress is . . .

Fred and I both wrap our arms around her and say, "*We* love you, Kenney."

"Hey." Neila is suddenly standing in front of us, with Grant. "Can we join your little love-fest or is this a private function?"

"Come one, come all," Fred says. "Everyone is welcome. Bring the team. The only rules are that you all have to hug us." He holds out his arms in the direction of Grant.

Grant keeps his eye on me while he says, "Okay. I think I can afford that price of admission."

"Well, not me," Kenney says.

Neila sits across from me, and Grant sits between her and Kenney, across from Fred. Neila starts picking blades of green from next to Fred's knee. Her knuckles are brushed with chocolate-colored creases, little drawn-looking lines that spread a web across her palms. She's selecting the grass stems carefully with her thin fingers, pulling each cylindrical stalk from its sheath. Then she places the white-tipped tender end between her teeth, closes her lips around it, presses them together, and sucks in the sweetness.

"So what are y'all up to?" Grant asks. Something in his tone of voice makes me feel suddenly responsible for this whole gathering. I'm the one Neila invited to his party, and the way he keeps looking at me makes me feel uncomfortable and queasy, like he's expecting something more. I mean, he seems like a nice enough guy and all, and it isn't as if he's being *mean* or anything . . .

Finally, I shrug. "Same ol', same ol'," I say.

He bobs his head like one of those dogs people have on the shelf in the back window of their car. "Cool."

"Actually," Fred says. "It would *normally* be the same ol' stuff except that this time we're sitting by the *pond* instead of on the *swings*, while convincing Kenney how much we are devoted to her."

Neila fluffs her little pile of discarded, picked grass, then draws it up with her fingertips like she's pulling from a pile of powdered spice for some recipe. Slender sturdy fingers. Strong. "Is that so?" she asks.

"You must be Kenney," Grant says.

"Duh." Kenney rolls her eyes. "We've met."

"Oh, that's right," Grant says. "I was just so stunned by your glory last time that I forgot." He slaps his forehead.

Kenney laughs. "It's an honest mistake. It happens all the time."

"So," Neila leans closer to me and says quietly, "did your

parents survive the shock of having a dying guest at their table?"
She twiddles with a strand of grass, then gathers a pinch from
the pile and sprinkles it into her palm. Such green, green grass.

"Yeah, I think they'll be all right," I say. "How's your throat?"

"Back to normal," she says, then makes a little pig noise to
prove it.

"So," Grant says. "Neila and I were just talking about what
we were in our past lives. I think I was a monk."

Fred laughs.

"I was a sheep," Neila says.

"I was Joan of Arc," Fred says.

"I think you," Grant says to Kenney, "must have been a spin-
ster governess."

"Yeah, right," Kenney says. "Well, Aurin was a man who
cheated on his wife all the time."

"I was not," I say.

Neila tosses a handful of grass at me. "You were too," she
says. "I can see it!"

I duck my head back, squint my eyes. I try to catch the grass
ball that splinters into a thousand feathers and sprinkles into my
hair, down my shirt, catches in the creases of my pants, litters my
lap.

"Maybe you were a nun," Grant offers as an alternative for
me.

"All that chastity between the two of you has got to make at
least one of you a saint," Fred says.

"And we know which one you think it is," Kenney says.

I grab a handful of grass and throw it at her.

And now everyone is throwing grass. I roll onto my back,
shielding my face, as if grass is going to hurt. Then I sit up, adopt

piano-bench posture, hold my hand to my breastbone like my mother, and say, "Well, even us saints have to eat, and I'm getting hungry."

"Ugh," Kenney says. "Didn't we all just eat?"

"I didn't," Neila says.

Grant looks at her quizzically. "How can you eat right after practice?"

"Well," Fred says, "I, for one, have to watch my figure."

"Come on, Aurin," Neila says. "I'll take you." She gets up and extends her arm to help me to my feet.

I take her hand.

"I'm staying here," Kenney says.

Neila hoists me up.

"How am I going to get home?" Grant asks.

"We can give him a ride," Fred offers.

As we get up, Neila asks, "Wanna go to the Taj Ma-Teeter?"

We link elbows. "Of course I do," I say.

"But first," she says, "we have to get my video camera."

"What for?" I ask.

"We're going to make a movie."

And with that, we leave them behind.

She's wearing political buttons pinned to her guitar strap and her shredded black T-shirt, and holding together holes of her shorts. Her hair is short, mangled, and multicolored. Her teeth are crooked and chipped. Her voice is larger than her body has air to support it. The buttons say things like *Boycott Kmart, Save Pigeon River, Kindness Doesn't Kill,* and *I'm Sarah.* The guy playing bass next to her is tall and skinny with scraggly long hair. They must go to that hippie college, Guilford.

The woman stops singing.

"So you want to film me, huh?" She smiles.

I was afraid she would be angry, but she sounds nice. Friendly.

"I've just never seen a band in the grocery store before," Neila says. "What are you doing here? Did they hire you?"

"No."

"Do they even know you're here?" I ask.

The woman shrugs, plucks at a string, and twists a tuning knob.

"So, your name is Sarah?" I nod to her button.

She smiles and turns around to the guy, who sort of laughs, then says, "Mine too," as he points to the button on his T-shirt.

"It's a campaign against dissection," the woman says. "We're protesting by exhibiting solidarity with our sister in the force against The Man." She holds out her hand, "I'm Scratch."

If Kenney was here with us, she would be dying of embarrassment or finding a way to humiliate someone. I'm already involuntarily blushing from trying to have a seminormal conversation with these people who are anything but normal, except that in a way, they are. Normal, I mean.

"You're making a documentary?" Scratch asks.

"Sort of." Neila shifts her footing.

"It's about the grocery store," I add.

"Cool," Scratch says. "About the oppression of corporate headquarters and the way they infuse toxins in the very air we breathe, let alone the waxified vegetables and fruits they try to trick us into eating by genetically altering them and trying to pass them off with the mislabel 'organic'?"

"Something like that," Neila says.

The guy nods. "School project, huh."

"Sort of," I say. "Not really."

The guy's head is still bobbing. "I dig it."

"Great talking to you," Neila says. Maybe she's feeling as put-on-the-spot as I am, like we're taking up these people's important political statement time while we're just goofing off. She puts on her undercover movie spy voice, and says, "We gotta get going on our important, top secret project."

"I understand," Scratch says. "Peace out, sister." She flashes the peace sign to us, nods, then plucks a string and starts singing again.

*Standing in the grocery store,*
*throwing items in,*
*some people are cardboard,*
*some people in love,*
*forgetting their passions*
*letting new ones begin . . .*

Pretty folk-y tune, with a little funk thrown in from the guy's bass.

"Perhaps," I say as we're approaching the seafood section, "we should liberate these fish from their tanks." I zoom in on one glazed-over eye through its glass casing. The water is cold, murky, blue. The fish are huge and silver with black spots. Their pink gills open and close, open and close. Their eyes don't blink.

"We could strap our belts to the sides, and just carry them out like purses," Neila says. I turn the camera and zoom in on her eye. Lively, blinking, layered with depths. The amusement with our situation, the pleasure, joy, laughter. The part I can't figure out yet. The fun of being with her and the extra part that makes this seem different somehow. The part I can't see, but know is there somewhere.

"I really am starting to get hungry," I say.

"Me too." She places her palm flat on her belly.

"The sound of your voice makes me think of rocks," I say as I toss some tofu into the shopping cart.

Neila grabs the kale. "That's because I swallow handfuls of gravel every day. Of course, I have to mix it with sugar to help it go down."

"I see," I say. "Is that how you got such a lovely gizzard?"

"Yes. But I have to spit out the extra pebbles. You know, extract the larger bits from filtered sand. Gotta be careful with water, though—it'll make my throat into concrete." She puts some tomatoes into the cart.

"What do you do with the extra pieces?"

"I make a wall for you and your friends to sit on top of and watch Frisbee." She starts laughing and my face flashes a bit of embarrassed red.

"Be careful not to laugh too much," I say, "or all of the gravel will spill out and scatter like marbles across the floor." I flip a bulb of garlic into the basket and it rolls along the metal grate. "Then we'll slip and fall."

"We should put the gravel thing in our movie," Neila says.

"As a cartoon sequence," I say. "With ballooning music that has trombones and accordion. And our drawings will dance and float across the air. We'll be far more graceful than in dance class."

"Everything will be in muddy tones, except for the bright bits that are us. We will look like stars."

"With your voice and my wall, together we'll be the queens of gravel, ruling over all the land, air, and water."

On our way out the door, Scratch and her friend are still singing. They wave.

# Making Things

Neila's house is immaculate. It looks like it belongs in *Architectural Digest*. My house is sterile with kitsch decorations, but hers has Taste. The living room has polished wood floors and a giant Persian rug lined with rich blue, gold, and white swirly designs splashed with specks of red. The couch is off-white, clean, streamlined. The end tables and coffee table are matching beige wood, glass, and brushed matte metal.

She plops her bag containing the video camera onto the couch, then grabs my hand and pulls me toward the kitchen. "Come on."

We're laughing and tripping over our feet as the plastic bags rustle and sway and bang against our hips.

We clomp the groceries onto the counter, and start unloading foods. I rinse off the kale while Neila pulls out the tofu, and starts crumbling it into bits for broiling. She takes a chunk and slimes it onto the back of my neck.

My head shrinks into my shoulders while my muscles dance around the cold slimy clump of tofu in Neila's hand. I shake a shower of water droplets from the kale onto her face.

"Hey," Neila says. "Do you think they thought we were a couple?" She asks this like an afterthought, or a continuation of a conversation we were already having.

"Who?" I'm still laughing and my skin is still squirming, and now my head is getting dizzy and a thousand prickles of cold and hot are pulsating all over my skin and in and out of my body.

"Scratch and that guy."

"Oh, them." I shrug. "Well, they *did* play that love song as we were leaving." I laugh. Her question makes me nervous. "Why?"

"Did you know Grant has a crush on you?"

Oh, is that what her question was about? Like . . . am I free to date her *cousin?* Maybe that's what she was going to tell me at the party. My stomach isn't feeling so good right now, a little puke-ish. "No," I groan. "How come?" I sound like I'm whining and wailing the big question "Why?" to the universe. This moment is like all of the injustice in the world getting dumped on me simul-taneously. It's as if I'm in a secretary movie where I'm trying to get to work on time, and have to run through mud puddles that splatter all over my ankles, then scuff my brand-new patent leather pumps. And before the elevator reaches my floor, it jars to a halt and I spill coffee all over my white blouse. Still determined to pull myself together, I hitch up my sagging panty hose and poke a big giant hole in them, causing a run all the way up. Then everything pauses, leaving the camera to hold its focus on me in the stillness with a "Why me?" expression on my face. I feel like Kenney.

"It's not such a bad thing," Neila laughs at me. "My cousin isn't the worst that could happen to you."

"I know," I whine. Melodramatic.

"Come on, Aurin, most girls would kill to be in your posi-tion."

Why is she doing this to me?

"It's because you're so cute," she says.

"That's why you're torturing me?" I ask.

"No. That's why he likes you."

"And I'm not cute," I say.

"Oh yes you are," she says. Then to add more torture, "It's the dimples in your cheeks when you smile, and the way your eyes are shaped to point up at the corners."

I cover my face with my hands. How incredibly embarrassing.

"And the line of your profile," she traces her finger lightly down the bridge of my nose, "and the way it curves into the dip right above your upper lip . . ." Her finger pauses ever so slightly.

I take in a shallow breath, but draw it out to make it into a slow deep breath, to quell the sparkles of glitter confetti fluttering around in my belly, swirling like a snow-dome's storm, and settling in my lap. I hold my head as still as possible.

"Is nice," she concludes, then pulls her hand away from my lip, and turns back to the tofu crumbles.

I pull my lip into my mouth and wet it with my tongue, where her finger was resting just a moment ago. I must totally be going crazy. I can't tell if she's hitting on me or trying to test me for Grant's market.

I can't look at her. I de-focus my eyes on the kale leaves, which are a blur of dark green as I pull off the leaves, and shred them into a pile in a stainless steel cauldron she has set on the counter. My cheeks are still hot, but I can look at her again.

Her head is bent down, studying the marinade she is mixing for the tofu.

"You do this often?" I ask.

"What's that?" she asks, flinching slightly. "Oh yeah." She inhales. "All the time." She exhales. "I'm going to be a master chef."

"Hi, girls," a voice comes from the kitchen's doorway. I turn to see a slender, polished woman. Her deep black hair is pulled back like an oil slick, and knotted into a sculpture covering the crown of her head. Her delicate features are slightly exaggerated, her eyes rounder than I usually see on people, her lips bigger than Neila's, her smile wider. She's a taller, more graceful, more intimidatingly elegant version of Neila.

"Hi, Mom," Neila smiles. "This is my friend Aurin. We're making dinner."

"I see that." She arches her groomed eyebrows and looks down the length of her nose at us, regally.

"And we made a movie today."

"Oh?"

"Aurin's going to be famous," Neila tells her mother.

"Is she now?"

Neila nods. "Up until today she was the only director on earth to have made the entire movie of her life without film or camera. But after today . . . well, her life has already begun to change."

# Heat Demons

In my movie I'll be elegant, long, and graceful. I will flow with the music, floating on the air like Ginger Rogers. Maybe even Fred Astaire. Why can't I be Fred? Why does Fred always get to be Fred? So there I am, Fred Astaire, and the music is melodious, and I'm dressed up in that suit like . . . Marlene Dietrich. And everything is beautiful and lovely. Everyone clears the dance floor to make way for us in our *Holiday Inn*-esque finale. Sweeping long flowing skirts with lots of white fluffy gauze. Sequins strategically placed, to glint from my hair or the corner of my eye or mouth. At first the picture is in black and white, but slowly color bleeds in and saturates the film, and everything becomes green and blue and aquatic. Then you realize I'm in a dance studio, not really a ballroom hall, and not even dressed up to look fancy. Crepe paper is everywhere. And when there is enough color, you can see that my hair is a mess, people are clearing the way because they're afraid I'm going to bump into them, and I'm stepping on everyone's toes.

Oh yes! This is a coordination-free zone! There is a lot of stepping on Kenney's toes today, since Fred isn't here to dance with her. And I'm a hopeless mess without Neila to dance with. She didn't say anything about not coming, so my mind keeps making loops around itself trying to think of why she isn't here. And so here I am, moving the wrong way the entire time, Kenney getting mad and frustrated at me and my lack of grace.

"Aurin," she mutters through clenched teeth. "Why don't you just stop it?"

I look at her quizzically. "Stop what?"

"You are making a fool out of yourself."

Oh, this from the person who practically begged me to join dance class.

She smooths her face over again, back into a smile, to keep up appearances for the sake of any potential onlookers.

"Okay," I say and let go of our stance, dropping her hands. I step back. "I'm stopping."

Her eyes widen, like I've splashed water into her perfect, pretty face. "Where are you going?" she asks.

"Bathroom," I say. Always my convenient excuse. In the movie, I would definitely have people go to the bathroom. You never see people go to the bathroom in soap operas, for instance, yet you follow every moment of their lives. I keep wondering how they can go through several days of amazing drama without once peeing. No. There will definitely have to be bathroom scenes.

"Hey." Kenney grabs my sleeve. "Class is almost over. Can't you wait?"

I fold my arms and stand there, looking at her.

"What?" she asks.

What I want to say is obvious: *Must you control every moment of my life? Dictate my every move? Every instant. Every day.* Instead, because I don't want to make a scene, because we never actually fight, because I don't even know what would happen if I were to retaliate against her, I don't say anything.

"It seems," our instructor says, "that we are having some difficulty over in the corner." The whole class turns their beady little eyes on us.

"Sorry," I say. "I lost the beat."

Kenney and I reposition.

"That's all right." Margaret emphasizes the *ll* and *ri,* drawing the words out longer than necessary. She holds her watch up in a dramatic posture. "Time's up anyway. You've all done swell today." She beams her bright smile at us, so proud of her students. She starts to clap, indicating that we should all join in congratu-lating ourselves. I wonder what this woman's life is like outside of class, what's important to her, if she has a family, or what she does in her spare time. I can't imagine that we, a bunch of uncoordi-nated teenagers and a variant group of slow old people, could possibly give her so much pleasure. What about her career? Didn't she want something more than this? I'll bet she drinks.

I have to wait for Kenney because she's my ride home, but I also have to get out of this room. I grab my bag from the floor by the coat hooks and whisk out the door—the most graceful move-ment I have made all day. I'm taking the gray-painted cement floor in the hallway in long strides, as if it's stairs that I'm scaling in twos. The vacuum of cold air jumps back from my face when I open the glass doors, and a wall of heat smacks up against me, shoves its way through the doors, pushes against the cold. The air currents are cartoons of demons and angels fighting one another. The puffy white cloud of coolness spreads its arms to catch the angry orange-yellow fire-y rascal of heat. The prickly claws get absorbed in the puff. The cold air hugs the heat, envelops it, squishes it down into submission.

The doors close behind me, and a tiny fluff of cold grabs at my ankles, tries to pull me back in.

"Hey, Aurin!" Fast feet, short breath, and super-calm voice are behind me. "Wait up!" I detect the slightest hint of strain there. But not much. Neila.

I can't stop the smile that teases my face as I stop walking to turn around. She looks slightly winded. I totter on the edge of where the sidewalk becomes curb, and dips into the hot black asphalt parking lot.

She slows down when I turn around. Then she stops walking and stands about four feet away. Too far by social space laws.

"Hey, where were you?" I ask.

"Oh, dance?" Neila wrinkles up her nose. "I keep forgetting. Those guys always talk me into playing Ultimate." She waves her hand to dismiss the building behind us.

A rock sinks into the pit of my belly. "Oh."

"I was just wondering," she says. She stands there, shifting her feet, then grasping the back of her head. The pose of an awkward statue. She changes position again, moving her feet forward a little closer in the immense personal space gap that's been left. I inch forward a little too, not wanting her to be left way out there in the distance. Now we're standing a little too close. She grabs a spring of her hair and pulls on it. "Just wondering," she says.

I step back a bit so we can both breathe a little better.

"Yeah?" Listening sounds. Waiting to hear her.

"What're y'all doing after?" she asks.

I shrug.

"Me and Grant were talking about getting some lentil burgers at Hong Kong House."

"Well you know," I say. I draw out the last word, I hold my jaw in a paused position while my eyes dance toward the sky and I knock the idea around in my head a little. My mind is leaping about like crazy. "I *love* Hong Kong House," I say. Avoiding eye contact with her, I drop my head back down to the ground. I kick my toe at a rock that's wedged in the sidewalk crevice. "I think

Kenney might just take me home, though. She's mad at me again or something."

"Grant's talking to her right now," Neila says. She places her hands on her hips, then quickly moves them again to cross her arms. She changes her clasp from her forearms to her shoulders. The grasp is too tight, so she moves her arms back to the hip position again for a brief moment. She finally settles upon putting one hand in her back pocket and hooking the thumb of her other hand through one of the belt loops of her cut-off khaki shorts. "If she doesn't want to go, we can probably give you a ride."

My eyebrows leap up. "Okay."

Wisps of cold air brush my skin like fingers lightly touching my arm hairs, neck, and cheeks. The glass doors are folding in together behind Kenney and Grant. Kenney is wearing her creamy vintage-peach dress with fingery veins of orange-red spidering across the fabric into line-drawn flowers. Her hair is somehow perfect again. Each swirl is placed exactly where it belongs. A few cup around her shell-pink ears. Others toss waves up and back away from her forehead. "Hey, sugar plum." Kenney plants a kiss onto my cheek as she tosses one arm around my shoulders and squeezes my wrist with the other hand. "You wanna catch a bite?" I must have been dreaming.

"What about that guy?" Grant says, lurking slightly away from the group. Skinny with hunched shoulders. A flap of hair smacking his eyelids. *So* affected.

"Fred?" I ask. *You know his name. Don't pretend like you don't know his name because you're too cool to remember it or something.*

"Yeah," he says. "How come he didn't show?"

I shrug. "Must've had something more important to do."

"I'll call him to meet us there," Kenney says. She digs her

keys from her gigantic red courier bag, then pulls her cell phone from the side pocket. What a Girl Scout: always prepared.

Kenney and I pile into her Mustang while Grant and Neila get into his slate blue VW Squareback.

"Yo, Fred," Kenney's saying as we pull out of the parking lot. She holds the phone with her left hand, and uses the right one to steer *and* to shift. I try to pretend that this doesn't make me nervous, but it always does. I just clench the window frame and look out the window.

"You will never believe it, but guess where we're going?" She's bragging. "No no, you're going there too. Meet us at Hong Kong . . . Now . . . Yeah . . . Meet us there." Her thumb presses the phone off, and she reaches behind her seat to toss the phone into her bag. Then she shifts into third. "I can't believe it."

"What's he doing?" I ask.

"Sleeping. Watching TV. What a loser."

"Did he say why he wasn't at class?"

"Didn't want to come. Forgot." She downshifts for a turn.

*You know, Kenney, you can't just keep treating your friends like this.*

"He is going to shit his pants when he sees that Grant is there." Laughing. Pleased with her private secret against Fred. "You should have seen him, Aurin. Grant was all like, 'hey, um,' shuffle shuffle, 'you want to come with Neila and me to get something to eat?' Like he was flirting with me or scared of me or hitting on me or something."

"Cool, Kenney. Real nice."

"Well, I can't help it, can I?" She's still laughing. "What am I supposed to do? Make every guy Fred falls in love with turn out to be gay? Puh-leeez, Aurin! I can't help it if guys like me."

"You are so full of yourself."

"You would be too, if you were me."

"Ha. Ha."

She slows down, shifts into reverse, drapes her arm across the back of my seat, twists her head around to parallel park. She's wearing sunglasses, and I didn't even notice.

*Kenney, do you ever wonder why we're even friends?*

I unbuckle my seat belt. I am tired. Exhausted. I'm always worn out from all the energy it takes to clench my teeth, bite my tongue, hold myself back from her. I pull out some extra vibrance from somewhere deep inside, a silk scarf thread I always have poking up like Kleenex, linked to a ball tucked into the hidden reserve. I open my door and step out onto the sidewalk.

A dull meow comes from the bench under the window, next to the front door of the restaurant. Fred is tired as well. "So what's up?" he asks. "What's the deal?"

Kenney flashes a smile at him. "You'll see."

Fred gets up and we follow Kenney in. She swishes and sways past the counter and clomps up the stairs to the booths.

# Rock Stars

Grant and Neila are already there, on either side of the table. I sit next to Neila, since she's on the side facing the door.

"I have a thing about seeing who's coming in," I explain to them.

"Me too," she says. "I heard somewhere that you should always know where your exits are."

Kenney leaps into the booth beside me, squishing me into Neila with her bony butt. So Fred sits next to Grant, not that he minds.

Grant nods to Fred. Dude.

Fred: "Wassup?"

"Lentil burger time," Neila mimics a muffled cheer, bops her head to the rhythm of the lentil burger theme music she's created in her mind.

"Is it the lentil burger song?" Fred asks.

Neila smiles, opens her lips wide. "Yeah. You know that one?"

"I sing it all the time," Fred says.

"What are you talking about?" Kenney asks, tapping the edge of her menu on the table and leaning around me.

Neila's eyes fall to the table. Her smile becomes more like a smirk. She reads her menu.

"You don't know?" Fred leans back, clasps his hands behind his head.

"It's world-famous," Grant says.

I stare down at my menu. "Number one on all the charts."

"Since when do you know about song charts?" Kenney elbows my upper arm.

"Lentil burger, lentil burger . . . Lentil burger time," Neila sings.

"It's kind of repetitive," Fred says, "but once you get it in your head, you can't get it out."

Grant says, "Catchy."

I say, "All the rage."

"Okay, I see," Kenney says. "You're messing with me."

And the meal goes pretty much like that, us making jokes, Kenney not getting them. Fast-forward and you see flashes of Grant leaning over the table, brushing his fingertips across my knuckles, Neila's cheek, Fred's elbow. Glint of Neila's smile flashed at Grant, cutting her eyes in Fred's direction, bumping her knee against my thigh. Fred leaning back, constructing seated dance moves, pretend disco, rolling his napkin, unfolding it and placing it on top of Kenney's head. Me tipping back my glass, crunching ice cubes and spitting them back in, then swallowing them and tapping the bottom of the glass to make sure it is empty. Kenney balling up her napkin, pulling off bits, slowly tearing it into shreds.

"We should have a band," Grant says.

"Oh yeah," I say. "A cover band where we do lounge versions of heavy metal and rap songs."

Fred croons, "I want some booty," Frank Sinatra style.

Kenney rolls her eyes. "I gotta get home soon," she says.

"Since when?" I ask.

"Yeah, what do you have to do today?" Fred asks.

"I have things to do," Kenney says, "that are important. And at the very least, mildly entertaining."

"I see," Fred says. "Don't let us hold you back then. I'll take Aurin home."

"Fine." Kenney digs in her bag, pulls out a handful of bills. She places the clump of money on the table. "That should cover it." She takes out her sunglasses and puts them on. "I'll see you later," she says from behind the darkened shield between her eyes and us, then turns around and goes. She swishes and sways between the tables, then clomps back down the stairs, in a restrained manner, toward the door.

Something about this scenario feels familiar to me. Even though I'm used to Kenney being dramatic, I haven't seen her act this way in front of a group of people in a long time. It almost seems like she's jealous, but I'm not exactly sure of what or who.

Fred and I turn to Grant and Neila. None of us says anything for a moment, like we've all been slapped and aren't sure how to respond, or which one of the collectively slapped should speak first. Finally Grant asks, "What's with her?"

I shrug, try to cover. "Always like that."

"Yup," Fred nods in agreement.

Neila scrunches up her forehead and takes in a few short breaths like she's going to say something, but then doesn't. Her eyebrows furrow in a mixture between annoyed and confused. "Hm," she finally says.

"Come on, let's go," Grant says.

Thud. Land on a dull note.

We all divide up the check and go.

# Skinny. Dipping.

The sky is starting to get navy blue, and we're all at the park. Again.

Fred and I are having to make up with Kenney. The rules of this ritual include pretending that she isn't really mad at us.

The towering lithium lamps are beginning to shine their orange pools of spotlight on the sand-mixed-with-black-grass-and-cedar-chips ground. Kenney is splayed atop the igloo-shaped jungle gym. Her long, skinny legs don't appear exactly graceful in this position as she looks like she's about to do the crab-walk. Fred is hanging from his knees, upside down, from one of the jungle gym's bars. His white T-shirt is tucked into his jeans, his arms dangle down, and his fingers brush tracks into the sand beneath him as he gently swings back and forth. I'm sitting on a bar near the bottom, facing in toward them, my arms hooked around two of the triangulated support beams.

The air is still sultry. Hot, wet, thick, and sticky. Like Jell-O. If I let go of the bars, I could swim through the upside-down fish-bowl made by the igloo.

Fred is humming to himself. Muttering, "Bored-bored. Bored-bored. Bored. Bored. Bored."

Kenney is sighing. She picks up one heavy hand and makes an attempt at fanning herself. Sweat beads are gathered above her upper lip, and congregating in the ditches of her clavicle.

The bushes rustle behind me, footsteps swish through the grass and kick through the sand with scrape-y sounds. I look up to Kenney for a cue first. She cuts her eyes indifferently to the side, toward the approachers behind me. Then she tosses her head back up, toward the sky, and continues fanning. Fred steadies from his sway and firms up his fingers, straightens his palms perpendicular to the ground. His biceps become taut and he disengages his knee-hold to straighten his legs into the air. He lowers his arms and slinks through the bars, carefully placing his feet on the ground and standing up, in one fluid motion.

I push my body out through the empty triangle of bars and lean back to see who is there.

My eyes run from yellow springs to placid milky caramel forehead to black and silver video box to bright upside-down smile and graceful neck. I quickly pull myself upright and turn my head around to face her right-side up.

"Hey, what's up?" Neila nods her chin back in an upward motion.

"We're just sweating to death," Kenney says. She turns her face away from the camera and holds up her arm to block the view of her head. "You?"

"Me and Grant were just gonna kick it back here a bit. We didn't expect you to be here." Neila lowers the camera and lets it dangle in her palm beside her thigh.

Kenney drops her arm block and faces Neila. "Perhaps you should begin expecting it," Kenney says, like we're a gang or something and this is our territory.

"Um, yeah. Okay," Neila says.

Kenney shrinks slightly. She tilts her head down, a wilted flower. Then she readjusts her palms and rolls her shoulders, and tosses her head back toward the sky.

"Feeling snappish?" Fred says, then changes character. He turns to Grant and does the guy-nod. "Hey."

Grant is standing in Neila's shadow, cast from the lithium light. He nods back at Fred. "So, is this a private party?"

Kenney shrugs. "It's a free country." Bristly.

Neila climbs into the bars and sits next to me. She wraps the crook of her elbow through a bar for support and props up the camera.

Grant crawls through to the middle and grabs the bars, under the space left by Kenney's knees. She scoots aside and spider-crawls down the side of the igloo, away from the rest of us. Fred is leaning into his own hold from inside the igloo's cage. Grant lifts his feet from the ground and dangles in the center of the apparatus. Silence.

"It's pretty hot, don't you think?" Neila says.

"No shit, Sherlock," Grant says and laughs at his lame cliché.

Fred, Kenny, and I nod. None of us says anything.

"We could go swimming," Neila says.

"Where?" Kenney sounds not quite as profoundly bored, though still slightly irritated.

"There," Neila points to Bristol Lake.

"Yeah, right," Grant huffs.

"It's all dirty," Kenney says.

Neila slides through the bars and stands inside the jungle gym. She smacks Grant's arm, points the camera at him, and says, "Come on."

Grant releases his grip from the bars, then follows Neila out through the triangular hatches. "Lemme see that." He grabs the camera out of her hand.

Fred quickly follows them. Kenney is looking out toward the sky, away from us. I wiggle from my bar after them. My feet sound a little too eager, making their fast sounds. And at the same time I feel hesitant, since Kenney doesn't seem to be following.

Neila and Grant have already reached the water's edge, and Fred is right behind them. I don't want to leave Kenney behind, but I also want to go to the lake with the rest of the group. I look back and see Kenney sauntering toward us, as if she's just come up with the idea to wander to the water's edge, and would be surprised to see us there. She meanders, stopping to inspect a tree's leaf or a blade of grass.

Her demeanor causes me to look away. She's being too theatrical, and it makes me lose any sympathy toward her, since her reluctance to join us is her own.

Neila pulls at the bottom edge of her brown-and-orange striped tank top. Grant throws his T-shirt from his body and jumps out of his shorts. He tosses the camera onto his pile of clothes, and is quickly in the water. Fred sits propped against a tree, untying his black patent-leather shoes. Neila peels her tank top upward. A shiny silver barbell stud shines from her belly button. I can feel the blush leaping in my cheeks and look away.

"You coming?" Neila says.

I look back at her, standing there in her navy blue flowered granny skirt and hot pink zebra-striped bra. I shouldn't be looking. It feels too private. I nod and step on the heel of my red canvas sneaker.

Fred is in ice blue and white snowflake boxers, jumping into the water. Grant splashes him.

Kenney comes up behind me and places her hand on my shoulder to steady herself while she removes her shoes.

Neila turns to face the water as her skirt slips past her hips and slithers to the ground.

Neila turns to face the water as her skirt slips past her hips and slithers to the ground.

"So," Kenney says. She hooks her fingers in the heels of her shoes and carries them toward Fred's pile to drop them down among his things. Then she lifts the corners of her skirt and walks in the water to her knees.

I take off my sun yellow T-shirt and khaki shorts, and stand there, feeling self-conscious in my economical gray cotton bra and men's boxer briefs. The summer's night air feels warm and cool at the same time, like silk on my skin. The water is warm as bathwater on my toes. This makes me walk more quickly toward Neila, who is already up to her shoulders in water. The moon shines through the trees lining the lake and drops slices of silver onto the water's surface which reflects onto Neila and highlights the smoothness of her skin. The deeper I get into the water, the slower I'm able to walk. By the time I get up to my waist, the water is colder on my feet, but the top is still sun-warmed.

Grant shifts his splashing from Fred to Neila. He hits her with a wall of water. A few sprinkles hit me, and they're warm.

"Hey!" Neila laughs. "Bastard." She hits him back with a smash of water.

Grant throws his arm around the back of her head and dunks her face in the water, then lets go.

Neila resurfaces, a glitter of water shining in her halo. Her face sparkles from droplets. After catching her breath, she smiles wide and says, "Asshole."

Grant grins back at her. Then they both turn to me and suddenly I am completely soaked. Cold water swirls up past my knees and warm water engulfs my shoulders. Cold water needles shoot at various parts of me, and when I can breathe air again, I feel a dance of water temperatures playing all over and around my body. I look at both of them momentarily, then dunk myself under again.

"This feels really good," I say.

Fred splashes Grant again, then swims off a little farther into the lake. Grant follows.

We have moved a bit from the shore. Kenney is all the way at the edge, still standing in water that only reaches her knees, like a bird. It's hard to tell what she's looking at.

If she ever let me make a movie with her, I'd put her on the beach. She'd be wearing a bedazzled pink tutu and a mango colored velvet bustier. She'd be standing at the edge of where the water crawls up, but doesn't quite lick her ankles. She thinks she's in the center of the camera's focus, so she's posing, but the lens pans out and moves her toward the corner of the screen, way in the back, a blurry, pink and orange dot like a little bit of flame or ashy cigarette tip. And then you'd realize that this water she's standing by and using as her background, this water which is really the foreground, it isn't even the same water that I'm in.

And because this is real life, I let Kenney fade into the distance.

Neila swims in toward me and brushes her hand around my waist. "Wanna dance?" she says.

Saffron bubbles swirl in my belly and make my mouth smile. I don't have control over the way my eyes dart away with my face, then trace back to find hers.

Neila giggles.

She puts both of her hands on my waist and moves my hips in closer to hers. Heat radiates from her thighs, making mine burn. Another current of water swooshes through, with the tiny movements made between Neila and me. My fingers are cold. My throat is dry, and I shouldn't drink the lake water.

"There are many kinds of dances you can do in a lake," Neila says. "Water ballet, for instance."

Her body is close to me, and I'm trying not to concentrate on the places where her skin touches mine. But all I can feel is the million little points of molecules where our bodies make contact. The dulled sharp edge of her hipbone bumping into mine, the rounded hard smoothness of her knee, and the soft curved line of her breast brushing lightly against my own. Her face has become closer as well, and I don't remember seeing that happen.

I can't hear Grant or Fred or Kenney. I can't hear anything. Cotton invades my ears and throat.

Neila laughs, embarrassed. "Sorry," she says.

"What?"

"Are you freaked out?" she asks.

"No," I say. I search my head for a moment. I don't find anything. The only thing I have is this feeling. What is this feeling? "I like this," I say. Then I'm surprised.

Neila leans forward into me again. Her hands are cupped into the small of my back, my arms slip easily around her.

"Um, Neila?"

"Yeah?"

"What about them?" I ask, though I'm not sure why. What just happened?

She moves back from me, but keeps a hand on my hip. We look for Fred, Grant, Kenney. Fred and Grant are on the shore, struggling their wet bodies back into their clothes. "Hey!" Grant shouts. "Come on! We're ready to go."

# Family Feud

**Kenney left us, so Grant is driving everyone home.**

"So what were you guys doing in the water?" Grant asks.

"You're so nosy," Neila says.

"Dancing," I say.

Neila and I are in the backseat, stealing glances at one another with secret smiles, her pinkie resting on mine. Fred's in the front and looks like he's got something up his sleeve too, but I'm not sure what. And I don't mind so much that Kenney isn't with us.

"So what's going on up there, Fred?" I ask.

"None of your business," he says.

"Oh good! Looks like we've got a whole car full of secrets," Neila says. "Maybe we should make a game out of it." She pulls out her camera. "Twenty questions, anyone?"

"Is it bigger than a bread box?" Grant asks.

"Maybe." Neila says. She turns the camera on me. "I don't know if you can quantify it with a size."

"Too much confusing information," Fred says. "How about Truth or Dare?"

"I dare you to drop me off at my house," I say, since that's where we're headed. After all, my parents will be mad at me again if I'm out late *every* night this summer, and it's already getting late.

"What a spoilsport," Fred says.

Neila puts down the camera and yawns. "Yeah, I'm getting tired."

"Then I guess I should drop you off next," Grant says. "Then Fred and I can be the only ones in the car who aren't lame."

"Guess so," Neila says.

And then I'm home. I'm standing on my porch, and there is yelling coming from out of the house. Again.

The words "sick" and "tired" and "lazy" and "divorce" are flying out of my mother's screechy mouth. Nothing is coming out of Henry's.

I hesitate, but open the door anyway. A whole new world is on the other side. It's like I'm stepping into Narnia when I go home, only different.

"*There* she is," Prudence yells in a fakely delighted tone. "Our little princess has decided to finally return to her castle. Tell me, dear, did you have fun? I hope you did, because that's the last time you'll be going out for the rest of the summer."

"Now, now," Henry says in a quiet voice. "That isn't necessary. You don't have to get so worked up."

"There is nothing wrong with me!" she yells.

I head toward my room.

"Where do you think you're going? Doesn't your mother get to see her own children's bright smiley faces anymore?" She turns to her invisible advocate. "As soon as they become teenagers, they vanish. They are creatures of the night, returning to the home for free nourishment and shelter."

There really isn't anything more to be said, at least not by me, so I go to my room anyway. Her yelling gets dulled by the tuning-out mechanism in my head, and by the bedroom door I have closed between us.

"Hey, shithead," Shawn pops his head through the bathroom door that joins our rooms. "Don't tell them I'm here. Okay?"

"Whatever," I say.

"Listen," he says. "I'm going out. Turn on some music so they don't hear me, okay?"

"Yeah."

In my movie, the one where she's a shark, and Dad's in her stomach and Shawn's out somewhere surfing, they all start circling. I'm still wearing the business suit and faux pearls. My limbs flail wildly, making it look like I'm doing a twisted, manic dance. Bubbles float from my mossy head while the wool constricts and tightens around my skin. The pearls float with the bubbles and draw me toward the surface. You never see the blood. And the only sound is that fast danger music made with a variety of stringed instruments being scraped by metal forks and plastic combs. You can also hear Henry's bizarre electronics as the supporting melody. At the peak of the instrumental, when it's most intense, and before I reach the air, everything stops and there is just the blank, silent screen.

# Ice Cream

"Hey, is this where Aurin lives?" Neila whisper-shouts at my window screen. She's making fun of herself, shuffling her feet like she did the first time she came here.

My parents have moved their little tête-à-tête into the basement.

"Come on, hurry up." Neila waves me toward her. "I'm busting you outta here."

Am I imagining things?

"You're what?" I ask.

"No time for questions. Quick before they come upstairs," Neila nods her head toward the basement windows that are blazing with light and squabble-sound.

I grab a pile of clothes from the floor and throw them under my bed covers, just like a kid on a TV show. I don't know. I've never done this before, and of course the first thing that comes to mind is the cliché. So I turn out my lights and close my door, and tiptoe around the squeaky parts in the floor and quietly close the front door behind me, to meet Neila, who is waving me out toward the road.

We run and run and run to her car, which is parked a few houses down, and made invisible from our house by the trees.

We're still quiet and catching our breath after we've shut the doors and are already at the end of the street, turning onto the next one.

"What are you doing?" I ask.

"Taking you out for ice cream," she says.

"You are?"

"Well, I was stupid, and had some eggplant again, so my throat is itchy," she says.

"You're kidding," I say.

"Yeah."

We keep driving. I don't know what to say, partially because I'm embarrassed that she saw my crazy family situation. But also because I keep thinking about the lake. Plus, I'm incredibly aware of how she said *taking you out* for ice cream. I want to repeat it back to her like I'm in third grade and everything is somehow a double-entendre, like: *she said 'dixon' huh huh*. Then I notice that she's awfully quiet too.

"I wonder what Fred and Grant are up to?" I finally say.

Her shoulders relax as she smiles and shakes her head loosely. "I'm sure they've thought of something."

"I thought you said Grant had a crush on *me*," I say.

"Jealous?"

"No."

"That was just a cover," Neila says.

I want to ask who it's a cover for—the person Grant has a crush on, or the person who has a crush on me? But I'd be too embarrassed to find out if the answer was the one I didn't want.

"Hey, kidding aside, does Grant like Kenney? Or do you think Fred has a chance?" I ask.

"*Kenney?*" Neila says. "You've *got* to be joking."

"Well, I hear that sometimes people squabble and pretend to not like one another when they have crushes," I say. "Apparently boys do that all the time in elementary and middle school."

"Okay, Miss Developmental Psychology," Neila says.

"See?" I say. "Now *you're* picking on *me.*" I didn't mean to say that out loud.

Neila's cheeks brighten, but she holds her lips closed, trying to prevent a smile. She puts her hand up to cover her mouth.

"All I'm saying is, do you think Fred has a chance?" I ask.

"What do you think?" Neila returns.

"I'm asking you," I say.

She shrugs. We pull up to the Frosty King's drive-thru window. She orders vanilla in a cup. I get Rocky Road in a cone. Then we're quiet for the two or three minutes it takes us to get to the park.

Gravel crunches under our feet as we get out of the car and head toward the weather-worn gray wooden picnic tables at the edge of the parking lot. I tuck one of my legs underneath and let the other dangle over the edge of the table, swinging the heel of my foot against the bench. Neila sits the same way, but opposite, facing me.

"How's yours?" I ask.

Neila slides a spoonful of ice cream into her mouth and lets the spoon rest there for a while. She swallows. She shifts and her knee knocks against mine. "Good," she says. Then she wiggles her foot out from underneath and leans toward me to place the ice cream bowl on the table.

Her hair tickles my nose. I catch my breath.

She scratches her knee and picks up the ice cream dish again. Then, quicker than a lizard, so quick that I have to rewind and play it again to make sure it really happened, she darts forward, kisses my cheek, retreats, and returns to her ice-cream dish.

I cannot breathe.

Now I can't look at her, either, and start blushing. When I do look up, she is eating her ice cream as if nothing has happened, but squirrels are making busy in my stomach. She scoots closer to me, though her face does not betray anything. Then I see it, a glint of a smile stretching at the corner of her mouth, and it spreads and spreads until she is laughing. She moves her face closer, this time slow enough that I can see it. And she kisses me, releasing the butterflies in my stomach out into the sky. "That, by the way," she says, "was my secret—in case you were wondering." We kiss again, and finally all of those things that have been so busy inside of me are quieting down. Unbelievably, I'm not shaking as I thought I might, but instead everything is melting inside with all the ice cream dripping down the side of my cone, spilling over my hand, spreading sticky goo until I let go and throw the cone over the edge of the picnic table, out into the trees.

And just as quickly, Neila hops up and says, "We should go." A little piece of my heart gets snagged by her belt buckle, and flops to the ground as she pulls away. Gravel sprays loud from where her feet land, then sprinkles quieter and quieter until she's drifted back to her car, turning back once to smile and wave me to come along with her.

I remember to breathe and pick my heart back up from the gravel.

# Touching Ground, or Slamming into It

"You are *so* grounded," an elevated whisper-hiss strikes at me from the corner of the darkened living room. All of the lights in the house are off, but nevertheless, here's Prudence sitting up, waiting for one of her lovely children to come home. I know she's done it before, in a fit of paranoia, to catch Shawn stumbling home drunk. He got seven weeks for that one, but the grounding didn't ever take hold since he doesn't really put much effort into obeying anything.

"Who?" I ask. "Me?"

"Who else?" she asks. "Do you see anyone else sneaking around here?"

"To tell the truth, I can't see much of anything, with it so dark and all."

"Don't get smart with me, young lady."

This is the point where I'm supposed to retort, "I'm not," but also shouldn't, since that would get me in more trouble.

"And where have we been?" She folds her arms and peers down at me, her eyes two glowing emeralds blazing lasers of X-ray vision into the contents of my brain.

"Nowhere," I say. "I was just out on the back porch looking at the stars, you know. Couldn't sleep."

"That lie would have worked if I was either born yesterday, or hadn't been waiting up in the dark for the past two hours."

"Oh." Caught.

"So do you want to try again?"

"I went to see a friend."

"Is that so?" Prudence's eyes bore deeper. "I can't imagine who, since Kenney called here at least half a dozen times, and Fred the other half." She gives me just enough time to speak, but then cuts me off before I get a chance to start, and says, "Does any of this have to do with your brother?"

The appropriate thing to do at this moment would be to nod, get Shawn in further trouble, let him take all the blame, then go to bed unscathed.

"No," I say.

"So it *is* that new little friend of yours, then. Nellie."

"No."

"Kenney seemed quite worried about you when she called," Prudence says.

"Mom, first of all, who is Nellie? Second of all, what are you talking about? What did Kenney say?"

"You know perfectly well who I mean. That girl we had over for dinner the other night. We thought there was something suspicious in her behavior, with that half-baked story about allergies."

I stand here in front of my mother, closing one eye to flatten out my depth perception, to make the scene more like the cartoon it really is. She is a black-and-white drawing. Curly smoke is coming from her head. She has jagged eyebrows with one eye slitted-shut, and the other bulging out of her skull.

"You think we really bought that?" she's saying. "Please. I wasn't born yesterday."

"As you've already mentioned. I think we're both aware of how long ago you were born," I mutter.

"What?" Now the cartoon is getting colored in, with red.

Maybe I'm just looking for a fight. Why I would be doing that, I don't know. I usually try to avoid conflict like the plague, as evidenced by my restraint with Kenney, my placating Pru. Reflections of one another, now that I think of it. The movie would cut to a close-up of a photo album antiqued with sepia and tarnished silver. The album is opened to a page with an old photo of my mother in black and white and touched with brushes of pink. Photo bleeds into moving image, the surroundings become modernized, and now you can see that it's actually Kenney in the photo after all, wearing her old-timey thrift store finds.

"Aurin." Prudence snaps her fingers in front of my face. "Are you paying attention to me? I swear, half the time I think you're on drugs." Then she stops snapping and holds her hands up to the sides of her face. "My god! That's it, isn't it? That girl is selling you drugs. No wonder Kenney was so concerned. She just didn't want to tell me, poor thing. Didn't want to get you in trouble. Well, she certainly is a good friend, isn't she?"

"Mom, I'm going to bed," I say, and start to walk past her.

"Oh no you don't. You stay and talk to me."

"No one is selling me drugs, Mom."

"Not yet," she says. "But just you wait. They'll be wanting money from you in no time."

At this I turn around. I can't let her go on being delusional forever. Especially since the worst thing I've consumed in the past few hours has been ice cream. "I am not doing drugs," I say. "And if you want the truth, the only reason Kenney is worried about me is that she can't be around me every second of my life, controlling every moment that isn't controlled by *you*."

"That does it, young lady." Prudence stamps her foot and

points her arm in the direction of my room. "You go to your room now."

"Good," I say.

"I was only going to give you two weeks, but that smart attitude of yours is going to get you the rest of the summer."

# I'm So Dead

Speaking of dead things, I used to play this game called "dead turtle" when I was little. It was a version of tag where when you get tagged, you flop on your back on the ground and say, "Dead turtle, dead turtle."

So now I'm laying in my bed at six in the morning, dead turtle position, with my legs poked up into the sky as high as they will go and my arms extended to hold up the blanket fort.

My blanket is the firmament.

It's knit, and sort of like a cocoon right now. The holes let beams of dusky dawn shoot through. Even the blinds on my window, though they are black, leave spaces for stinging rays through the slats. For some reason, this neighborhood, this part of town, or maybe it's just my house, all of a sudden seems to have an inordinate amount of light. The street lights, traffic lights, parking lot lights, and neon signs from the nearby twenty-four-hour hamburger stand make it impossible to see the real sky from here when its supposed to be dark out. In my movie, this place is a cosmic dot. My room would be visible from space because it's so well lit. But of course if I were a UFO, I wouldn't land *here* for fear of hitting something. I think extra-terrestrials must definitely be smarter than moths. They wouldn't just drift toward any light source only to get zapped in the end.

In this dead turtle blanket fort, everything feels upside down.

The stars from the holes in my blanket are stabbing my eyes, and my arms and legs are beginning to tire, so I let down the fort.

Now I can finally see what a disgusting heap of filth my room is. It stinks from all the dust that blankets a layer of my world. I am the queen of my own pathetic world of gravel. The dust drifts through and gets spotlighted by all those light shards, then lands in clumps. My dust never has stage fright.

Okay, speaking of stage fright, I've been having a lot of that lately. For instance, how am I going to tell my mom what I was doing last night? "Hey, Ma, I wasn't out doing drugs, I was just kissing a girl." Like she'd really go for that one. (This is the woman who still thinks Fred could suddenly gain interest in dating Kenney or me.)

"Hey, dork." Shawn pokes his head into the room at this surprisingly early hour.

"Yeah."

"You look like hell." Brotherly love.

"Thanks."

He reaches up and tucks his fingers around the lip of the doorjamb, hanging in my doorway. "Hey."

"Yeah?"

"I can't believe *you* got caught last night and I didn't." He grins widely, pleased to have beat his uptight little sister in the trick-the-parents game.

"Yup." I nod.

"How much time d'they give you?"

"Till the end of summer," I say.

He sucks in his breath and makes a whistle sound. "Damn," he says. "You must have been ba-ad. Better start thinking up a good excuse. So, wha'd you do?"

"Just went out with a friend for some ice cream."

"Must have been *some* ice cream to be worth all that."

The little saffron bubbles sparkle up and tinge my cheeks with fire sparks again. "It was," I say.

# Inky, Like Fred's Pants

"There's someone here to see you." Shawn's at my door again, this time around noon. He nods his head backward. "That guy." Very descriptive, but I know who he means since there's only the one guy that's ever coming to see me.

Fred peeks his head around Shawn's shoulder. "Hey."

Shawn releases his hold from my doorjamb, and pushes himself away from the door. His pounding feet stagger toward the kitchen.

"Hey, kitty cat, sure is dark and gloomy in here. What are you doing?"

"Cleaning up," I say. I figure as long as I've got plenty of time to do it now, I may as well straighten out my room a little bit. Maybe it can buy some of my time back from Prudence, for good behavior.

"Cleaning in the dark?" Fred asks.

"Yeah, well, I can see enough to make piles out of the main pile. I can do the dusting part later."

Fred flicks on the light switch.

I squeeze my eyes shut. "How come you're here?" I ask. "Did Kenney send you?"

"I can't come over for a visit on my own?" He pouts.

"Sorry," I say. "Come sit down." I scoot over to make a space for him next to me on the bed, pat the seat for him. "I just figured since Kenney was mad at me, she's sent you to come spy. I'm getting so tired . . ." I say.

"Me too," Fred sighs. He leans his head back, and rocks it slightly back and forth against my wall.

I cock my head and prick up my ears. "What's up?"

"I don't like the way she's acting lately," Fred says.

"I thought it was just me," I say.

"I'm really getting sick of it," he says. "All the remarks and comments and stuff. Sometimes it just really gets to me, ya know?"

"Yeah." It's been a while since Fred and I have actually talked about stuff, instead of just shooting the shit. In fact, it's probably been never. I always assumed he talked to Kenney about the important things and that I was just around as an extra. I'm not sure exactly why I thought that. It isn't as if Kenney's the easiest person to talk to all the time.

"Half the time I can't tell if she's kidding anymore, or if she really just hates me, or is uncomfortable or something," he says.

"I think she goes too far sometimes," I say.

Fred lifts his head forward and shakes it. "That's what I've been telling myself. It's too much. This afternoon we were on Tate Street and some guys come walking by, and she elbows me in the ribs, and says, 'Did you see that dude? He was looking at you.' So they turn around and one of them says, 'I ain't no fuckin' pansy-ass faggot.' He's this tough redneck. And he says, 'If I was lookin' at you, it's 'cause I think you're queer.' So Kenney opens her big mouth and says, 'You got a problem with it if he is?' And surprise, surprise, the guy says, 'Yeah, I got a problem with it.' But his friend saves the situation by saying, 'Come on, dude, let's go.' So they leave. But Kenney could have gotten us killed, you know? She just doesn't think."

"Shit," I say.

Fred nods and we sit there for a moment in silence. He's smoothing this ink spot on his khakis. He licks his finger and leaves a small coat of spit on the tip, then rubs it into the spot.

"Were you scared?" I ask.

"What do you think?" His shoulders are rigid.

I nod and look back down at my hands in my lap.

"Fred, have you ever kissed a guy?"

"What difference does it make? I'm still gay."

"That's not what I'm asking," I say. "Okay, how did you first know you were gay?"

Fred shrugs his shoulders. "I guess it's something I always knew."

"Yeah, but no guy liked girls in elementary school," I say.

"Nah, it's something more than that," Fred says. "It's the way I feel when a guy I like pays attention to me—like Grant. Or when we'd play spin the bottle in middle school, and my heart would jump if it landed on a guy. Plus, I never think about kissing girls. And I always admire these guys, but am never friends with them because I'm too shy."

"You are *not* shy," I say. "You're anything but that. Besides, don't you think a lot of people are like that?" I ask.

Fred shrugs again. "Yeah. I mean, I guess everyone gets nervous around people they admire. Or we can all tell if someone's cute, no matter what gender they are. But I never really liked girls the way other guys do. You know Kimmie Chandler? Remember how she liked me that one time and we went out on that date a couple of months after I moved here?"

"Yeah."

"Well, when she tried to kiss me, it made me feel sick. And not a good kind of sick. Like when I think about Grant, I feel sick, but it's thrilling. It's like champagne bubbles washing through me. When Kimmie's lips came toward mine, I had to turn my head, and even though they landed on my cheek, I still felt icky."

"Kimmie's cute, though," I say.

"Objectively," Fred says. "But ever since that, we couldn't even be friends anymore."

I nod.

Fred smudges the ink spot farther into the thigh of his pants. "Yeah, I kissed a guy," Fred says. "I kissed Matt Derkins."

My head feels bright pink, cotton candy. "You did?" I whisper.

"Don't tell anyone, okay?" Fred doesn't even have to ask.

Matt Derkins is this guy that I haven't thought about in a while. He and Fred were in science together and were friends right when Fred first moved here, before the Kimmie incident. They used to study at each other's houses a lot. Matt had an acne situation, but was still kind of cute. No one really hung out with him much, but he was nice. When he moved away, no one really noticed. Plus, Fred never said much about it, just started hanging out with Kenney and me more often.

I'm still looking at Fred intently, the "Tell me" plea on my face.

Fred takes in a deep breath and lets it out slowly. "Okay. It's not much of a story here. We were in his basement, watching TV. We were supposed to be studying, but got distracted or bored or something. So we're sitting there and he's flipping through channels and everything is just commercials and he's getting nervous and fidgety and stuff, and is all like 'I'm sorry. Can't find anything to watch.' So I go, 'Well, let's just study then.' And he puts down the remote, but the TV is still on. It's QVC."

He stops in the way that sounds like the story is finished, which it can't be because he hasn't gotten to the good part yet. "And?" I say.

"So he looks at me and looks away and I think I know what he's thinking. Then he tells me that they're moving next week, which wasn't what I was expecting, so I say, 'Why didn't you tell me?' And he says he doesn't know, maybe because he wasn't sure if we were really friends, and because he likes me."

Fred is talking so fast it sounds as if he's already tape-recorded this part of the conversation. "And of course I go, 'Well, I like you too.' And he says that he doesn't mean just like that. He likes me more than a friend. And I can't believe my ears, and I'm starting to get an excited feeling in my chest. And he's apologizing and knocks over a Coke and apologizes more and reaches around me to grab this doily from the end table to soak up the spilled Coke."

Fred pauses again.

"Yeah?" I say.

"So as he's leaning over, I just kiss him."

"Whoa," I say. "Then what happened?"

"Well, we're kissing for a while, but all of a sudden his mom is standing there, and she says, 'What are you doing? Get out.' So I grab my book, but leave some homework there by accident, and go. I didn't go home right away, though. First I went to Bristol Lake for a while and just sat and freaked out and cried. The next day at school he just leaves my stuff at my desk in homeroom, but no note or anything. He wouldn't call me or talk to me all week and then he moved."

"Why didn't you tell us?" I ask.

"What was I supposed to say? I didn't know you very well and didn't have too many extra friends to spare. And then time just happened, and it never came up."

"Yeah," I say. "Um, Fred?"

He doesn't respond. He's just sitting there real quiet, smudging the ink spot into his pants.

"Don't do that, okay? You want some club soda or something to get it out?"

"Yes," I say.

"You don't even know what it is yet." She pulls out into the street. "But I like your answer." She cuts her eyes toward me, slips into a smile, and slides her hand onto my knee.

"So what is it?" I ask. Her hand is still there, making a thousand spidery circuits of orange and yellow buzz through my thigh.

"I need your directorial assistance," she says. "I'm painting my room and I'd like to have it documented."

After we pull up to her house, she hands the video camera to me, and we go directly to her room. The first thing I can see through the lens is that all of the furniture is pulled to the center and draped with sheets. Next I pan to the floor, which is covered with a clear plastic tarp and dozens of small paint cans and large cans and bottles and tubes and brushes and sponges.

"Wow," I say. "This is a lot of paint supplies."

"I need a lot of colors," she says. When she points at the walls, I turn the camera to find that she has drawn all over them with bubbles and fish and grass blades and water and rocks. The scenery blends into itself. The top half is fish so that everything else is underwater, though it looks like land. The overhead light in the middle of the ceiling is a giant sun, and stars speckle around the edges.

"I'm going to put up white string lights when we're done," she says. "And hang these." She floats a clear bowl full of plastic ᴴh in front of the camera.

I can't even imagine doing this to my room, even though it ᴴs so much like it could be scenery for my movie. I've been ᴴng my private vision inside of me for so long, like a tiny ᴴe egg buried deep in velvety cloth and protected by a

"I don't care. These are old anyway."

"That is so not true," I say. "Just hang on a second." I go to the bathroom and get the stain stick that I pilfered from Pru. "At least you can use this." I hand it to him, and he starts wiping it into the ink spot. "Neila kissed me," I say as casually as possible. As if it's nothing. As if it's this tiny piece of instructions he might need for removing the stain from his pants.

He doesn't look at me. Keeps smudging the stain stick. I'm standing in front of him, watching. He twists the cap back on and hands me the stain stick. I walk it to the bathroom, replace it under the sink, and come back to my room.

I stand there in front of him.

"So tell me about it." He sounds like he expected me to start spilling the story long before now.

"It could have been nothing," I say. I tell him about ice cream and how it happened and I'm talking really fast, not leaving a whole lot of room for breathing in between sentences, the whole story running together like Fred's only faster and more nervous and immediate, and I rush up to the end, where Neila walks back to her car and I'm sitting there on the picnic bench, and then I keep going and tell him to the part where I'm walking back to my house in a daze, and argue with my mother and get grounded, but how it was *so* worth it, and then Fred comes in and then since he knows the rest, I stop.

"It doesn't matter if it was nothing," Fred says. "Even if you imagined it, does the truth of your reality dictate that you wanted it to happen?" He sounds like someone else saying this. Like a therapist. "Even if it made you think about wanting it to happen, it matters, it was *something*."

I shrug. I'm scared because not only was the kiss the first real moment to define my feelings and give shape to my reality, but this is the first time I've ever talked about it with anyone, and now that I'm finally saying it, it seems even more real.

"I have a lesbian aunt," Fred says. His mood shifts up a few more notches. "After she divorced her husband, she became friends with this woman who asked her out for coffee." A smile winks into his cheeks. "She told us this story about how after she said yes, and she was walking back to her house, it suddenly dawned on her what "coffee" meant. And she smiled to herself, and thought, 'Yeah. I'd like some coffee.'" He raises an eyebrow at me. "So, Aurin. Are you ready for coffee?"

My eyes widen and I open my mouth. A cartoon. Nothing comes out. Then, "If I am, does it have to mean there's no turning back?"

"I don't know," Fred shrugs. "I read a lot of stuff with different opinions. What do you think?"

Now I'm crying. I don't mean to be, and it feels stupid. I'm standing in front of this guy with a big ink stain on his pants, this guy that's been my friend for three years, who I've never really talked to.

"Shit. I don't know."

Fred gets up to stand in front of me. "Well, you know, it might be fun to open new doors. You might not want to turn back. Jeez, Aurin, it's about *time. Go* for it. At least one of us ought to be having some fun." He reaches his arm around the back of my shoulders and pulls me in to him. "Your real friends will still love you."

I'm not sure anymore if that still includes Kenney. But now here's Fred hugging me close and tight against his horribly flat chest. I'm crying big inky tears that blur down my face and all over the front of his softly unsoft shirt.

## Jail Break

"Psst!" A spray of gravel sprinkles lightly against my windowpane.

I open the blinds.

"What are you doing in there?" Neila asks.

"Cleaning."

"Well, how much time you got?" she says.

"Until the end of summer," I say.

"Is that all?" Neila hangs her head dramatically. "I was hoping we could have more time than that."

"I meant how long I'm grounded." I press my face against the window screen, and when I see her standing there in the brigh late summer sunlight, wearing a fire-orange tank top and bag cut-off camouflage pants, I know more than anything else th am ready for coffee. I feel like throwing my head back and s ing, "Yes! Yes!" to the universe, but instead spread my arm and say, "For you, I've got all the time in the world."

"Well, good." She claps her hands together. "I was w if I could steal a little bit of that time, like perhaps th part before your mom gets home?"

"How delightfully sneaky," I say. "I'll be right o      s after I'm outside, "Of course I can't be too long i      fi calling."

"Ugh." Neila rolls her eyes. "How confining      loo out of here." She grabs my hand and we dash to      hol you to help me with something," she says wh      fragi cement-colored box. And now in seeing the contents of my head displayed on her walls, all over her room, she unlocks that box. "It reminds me of my movie," I say.

"It does?" She steps closer to me, and looks into the lens.

I focus on her eye. "I mean, because everything is underwater," I say.

She leans in and kisses my cheek. "Yeah."

The little egg inside of me rattles around and starts to break free from the numb zombie gray box.

She pushes the camera aside and brushes her cheek against mine. Her hair tickles my skin like angel feathers. The egg cracks the crusty surface and flakes of dust crumble off my box while little glowy-things, new and shiny and bright, burst through—so soft and smooth.

I let the camera fall from my hand onto some unidentified sheet-covered furniture. And Neila tilts her face into my neck. I can feel soft flutters tickling my throat, which sends shivers through my shoulders and tail bone, and she giggles. "Butterfly kisses," she says and bats her eyelashes. She takes my hand into hers and places it up to her fluttering eyelashes.

"It tickles," I say. Then I brush my eyelashes against her shoulder.

She giggles and says, "Stop it, you're making me weak."

I hold out my hand. "Do it again, do it again," I say, hopping up and down like an eager little kid.

This time she holds her face so close to mine, putting her eyelashes on my closed eyelids. I can feel blue electric sparks leaping from her skin to mine and back again, like the tiny fingers of capillaries connecting arteries to veins.

And this time, kissing her is like the sublime moment of free fall from a cliff of rocks with so much water and gravel below, when suddenly I can feel feathers breaking from my back, splitting open through my shoulder blades, and sprouting wings while her fingers are gripping my spine. I am dizzy from it, and from the wash of lava rushing through my bones and sparking white-hot cold that cools and splits and breaks open again with sparks of frozen fizzle warm.

And then I forget about the movie and painting. I forget my mom and being grounded. I forget about Kenney being mad at me or jealous or whatever. I forget everything. Everything else, except for this.

# Friends Share Laughter

"God, Aurin," Kenney is spewing hot vapors into my ear as soon as I answer the phone, and I don't even know why. Of course, she's mad at me a lot lately, so it could be anything. "Sometimes I really hate you." She sounds like she's got tears in her throat. "I thought we were friends."

"I thought so too," I say. Though I am taken aback, I make my voice remain calm.

"For someone who is grounded," Prudence sings from the hallway, "she certainly has plenty of communication with her friends."

"I thought you wanted me to talk to Kenney." I cover the mouthpiece as I shout this.

"Oh great, so you're only talking to me because your mother told you to?" Kenney says.

"No," I say. Kenney's the one who called me, but it doesn't seem appropriate for me to remind her of that.

Prudence says, "So you think people who are grounded should be just as free to do whatever they want as any other day?"

"That's not what I said," I say. "Here, do you two want to go ahead and talk to one another and leave me out of this?"

"Hey," Shawn pushes through the bathroom door. "I need the phone."

"Good," I say. "Kenney, I'll talk to you later."

The only thing I can guess is that Kenney hates me because I am spending enough time with Neila to get grounded for it.

And of course, the more aggravating part for her is the fact that she hasn't been included in any of it.

But just for clarification, Kenney shows up at my front door about fifteen minutes after we hang up.

"Kenney," Prudence says. "How delightful to see you. Why don't you come in? Aurin is in her room."

Kenney waves her hand in front of her face and makes choking sounds. "Ugh. What is this smell?" she asks.

"Dust," I say. "Believe it or not, all of this moving around of things stirs up a lot of sediment."

"Yeah, I guess you've been doing a lot of that lately."

"I suppose so," I say. She doesn't look as mad as she sounded over the phone.

"Aurin." She flops onto my bed. "What's going on? It isn't fair, you know. I always include you in everything I do."

"Hey, no one's stopping you," I say. "You're welcome to start cleaning my room any time."

"That isn't what I meant," she says, "and you know it. I want things to go back to the way they were."

"Kenney, at this point, I can't remember where they were, and to be honest, I don't think Prudence would like it very much if my room went back to exactly how it was before I started. She would think I hadn't done anything at all."

"So maybe you haven't done anything," she says. "No one needs to know. Things don't have to change." Then she adds, "And I wasn't talking about your room."

"I know," I say.

"So let's just make up and be friends."

If I've been a good girl and memorized my lines correctly, I'm supposed to say, *Kenney, we* are *friends*. But she's been mad at me so often lately that the accumulation of her anger hits me like a spike of steel gray irritation piercing my brow. So instead I say, "We can't." I shake my head. "It isn't that easy."

"What do you mean?" Kenney asks. "Of course it is. If you just apologize, I can forget everything and . . ."

"Apologize?" I ask. "Apologize for what?"

"For making plans with Neila and not including me so that I had to be on the sidelines like stale corn chips. For pretending to be cooler than me, even though we all know that it was *my* idea to take dance, and it was *my* idea to start hanging out with Neila and Grant for Fred. But now you've taken over. You're acting like you're the monster princess of the world. I know, I know, you probably just got caught up and forgot, or the timing wasn't right. But don't forget, I'm the one people look to for trends, and . . ."

"They do not," I say. "Kenney, who? Who are you referring to? If anything, they laugh at you." I didn't mean to say that out loud. Now I'm the mean one.

Her face hardens. Her eyes become little lumps of green coal.

"How could you say that to me? So you've just been hanging out with me for pity?"

"No," I say.

"And here, I thought we were friends," she says. "To think all this time I thought I've been the one helping you, when in reality you're just a coldhearted serpent getting ready to strike at me as soon as you've shed your old skin."

I'm not, I know I'm not. And yet still, I can't find it within myself to tell her why I've been so distant, why I haven't been including her in everything. I'm afraid that if I tell her, it'll confirm something she's suspected all along and either she'll be happy and that'll be good, or she doesn't really want to know the truth and she'll hate me for it. But either way she'll know, and it'll be solid. Either way, things will change forever. Though, in a way, I guess they already have. Besides, what if she somehow uses it against me?

I mean, I know no one really ever bothers Fred about being gay, but he's a guy. And as far as they know, he hasn't ever acted on it. But for this, I'd be getting more than one person in trouble. And I can't imagine what Kenney'd be saying about me, or how other people would react. But then again, why should it matter what people think?

"Kenney, you know that isn't true," I say. I am turned in on myself and quiet and guarded and vulnerable. She is standing like a pillar, her chin pointed to the sky, her eyes glaring down at me from her incredible height.

"What is it then?" she demands.

I shake my head. "No," I say. "Not when you're ordering me around like this. It makes me feel like too much of a child. And believe it or not, Kenney, you aren't my parent."

"Well, we're just spilling *almost* everything today," she says. "Aren't we then? Any more resentments you want to share with me? Let's see here. So far we've got . . ." She begins ticking them off on her fingers. "You don't like the way I talk to you, don't like being around me, feel embarrassed by my presence and my behavior, not to mention my clothes. Anything else? Don't you like my shoes? In general I'm just not good enough for you. Maybe not athletic enough? Maybe I'm too tall?" She narrows in her eyes for number ten, "We already know I'm the right gender for you, but I guess I'm just not *forward* enough."

My first instinct is to retort: *forward? You're downright pushy.* But underneath the words, I know what she's saying, and I can't escape from that. She must already know about me kissing Neila.

At this, I straighten my stance, take in a deep breath to make myself stronger. "No, Kenney. This isn't about you. I don't know exactly what it is, maybe a combination of things. But I know that Neila likes me and she doesn't treat me like an extra piece of crap laying around the attic. When we spend time together, we both have fun."

"Yeah, I bet you do," she says.

I am not backing down. "Yes," I say. "We do. And yeah I get nervous when I'm around her, but it isn't because I think she's going to get mad at me for not doing the right things. And it isn't because I feel like I have a certain image to uphold for both her and myself. It's just because I don't want the time we have together to end."

"Well," Kenney purses up her cheeks, sour sucking-lemon face. "Isn't that special?"

"Hey," I say. "This isn't about me and you."

"Nope," Kenney says. "Sure sounds like it's about me and her."

"It isn't that either," I say. "It's about me and Neila. There's room enough for me to have more than one person in my life. This isn't a comparison between you and her. What I have with her is a totally different thing. Kenney, you're my best friend."

"Correction," Kenney says. "I *was* your best friend."

"I admit, I haven't exactly been acting like a best friend lately, but that doesn't mean that I'm not allowed to be a butthead for just a few days. Please, give me a little leeway while I figure things out."

"You had time," Kenney says. "Didn't you figure anything out over the past few days?"

I nod my head.

"Well?" she asks. "What did you come up with?"

The incredible sound of the ticking clock. The movie scene would cut to a classroom with everyone taking a test and beads of sweat forming on their foreheads. Their pencils would be scratching fiercely, with amplified sound. The blurry background walls are pistachio pudding green. The clock face is huge and round and white with black numbers and long slender black hands.

"And?" Kenney has her arms folded, her foot tapping.

"I really like her?" I say.

"We *know* that," Kenney rolls her eyes.

"I mean *really*," I say.

"Aurin, come on and just say it. I want to hear it out loud from your mouth."

"I kissed her."

I watch Kenney's face turn to scarlet and crimson, snow turning pink from drops of blood. Her eyes well up with water, but not a drop of water spills over the edge. She turns around without saying a word. It strikes me as objectively funny that I've rendered her speechless, except that here she is, my best friend turning her back on me and walking out my door, saying nothing as she keeps on walking farther away.

I don't know if she's mad because it wasn't her that I kissed, or because she didn't get to have Neila all to herself, or if it's just because I didn't tell her sooner.

I pick up the phone, and dial Neila's number. I don't know exactly how she'll react, but I figure since everybody else in the whole wide world is mad at me anyway, I may as well finish the deal and make it *absolutely* everyone.

"Neila?" I say. "I told Kenney."

# What's the Big Deal?

Instead of talking on the phone, Neila comes right over. She throws a pebble at my window, like we're in a bad remake of *Romeo and Juliet,* and I go to the back door to let her in. It seems that Prudence has gone out to run her errands, so we've got some time.

"So what?" is the first thing Neila says. She flops onto my bed and curls her feet under while scooting her back up against my wall. "I told Grant," she says, then takes my hand and pulls me to the bed to sit next to her. She has her fingers wrapped between mine. "I'd tell everyone in the world if I could. It doesn't matter, Aurin. I really like you and I don't care what anyone thinks."

"You told Grant?" I say.

"Of course," she says. "He's my cousin."

"That must be how Kenney knew," I say. "No wonder she's so mad at me. I bet she thinks I'm withholding this information that everyone else knows about except her. She thinks she's being kept in the dark, and probably that I'm doing it maliciously."

"Are you mad?" Neila dips her head to find my eyes.

"No," I say. "But I am sad. I just lost my best friend."

She puts her arm around my shoulders and pulls me closer. "Oh, sweet," she says in the most comforting voice. (She called me *sweet!*) I'm beginning to feel giddy again, even though I should be feeling a lot worse about Kenney.

We're both quiet for a moment, then Neila says, "Remember that movie we were making?"

"Which one?" I ask.

"The one about my room," she says.

I can feel the blush running into my cheeks.

"Well, I can't find it," she says.

"Um, Neila?" I say. "When you told Grant about us, where was he?"

She's quiet again. I may as well be listening to the static-y dark electric buzz of telephone wire. "In my room," she says.

"You don't think . . ." I say.

"That he took the tape?" she finishes. "Well, it isn't in the camera."

"Has he ever mentioned hanging out with Kenney at all?"

"Well," Neila says. "He did say that they'd gone out yesterday. But I didn't think it sounded very important; he hangs out with a lot of people, you know. Plus, we'd all been hanging out as a group together."

"Except that Kenney was always acting weird and jealous," I say. "And she didn't call me yesterday, which is unusual since she calls *every* day. Of course, she usually finds it easier to forget me whenever there's a boy around."

Then there's a knock at my door. It's Fred. For someone who is grounded, I sure am getting a lot of visitors. He pushes his way through, grabs my shoulders and nudges me toward the bed while saying, "Aurin, you better sit down, because you are never going to believe this." My life is beginning to look more like a situation comedy than a movie.

Then he turns his head, "Oh, hi, Neila. I hope I wasn't interrupting anything." He looks a little flustered.

"No, it's cool," she says.

Then he flops onto my bed and holds the back of his wrist to his forehead in a dramatic fainting Southern belle posture. He takes in a deep breath and sighs.

"What is it already, wilting lily?" I ask.

"Which part do you want first?" Fred says. "The bad news, or the really bad news?"

Neila and I both say in unison, "The bad news."

"Oh, all right," Fred says. "But to save you, I'll give you the really bad news first. Are you ready?"

Neila and I both shout, "Yes."

"Grant," Fred starts. Then he sucks in his lips and fans his face. "Pardon me, I'm a little choked up. Aurin, honey, you got any water?"

I get him the cup from the bathroom. "Drama queen," I mutter as I hand it to him.

He takes a sip, puts down the cup. "Grant," he says again. "Kenney," he says. "Grant and Kenney," he sucks in his lips again.

"Oh, get on with it," I say.

"They're dating," Fred and Neila say in unison.

Fred turns his head abruptly toward Neila, who says, "Aurin and I had just started deducing that when you walked in."

"Already?" I ask Fred. "I mean, this is kind of sudden, isn't it? Besides, I thought they didn't even like each other."

"Maybe they're not officially a couple," Neila offers. "They only went out together once."

Fred looks like a crumpled empty paper bag.

"Oh, Fred," I scoot closer and put my arm around him. "I'm sorry," I say.

"Well, it wouldn't be so bad," Fred says, "if he hadn't led me on."

"What do you mean?" I ask.

"That night we all went swimming and dropped both of you off, Grant and I had a really good, long talk about me being gay and he seemed so open-minded about it and even said he wouldn't totally rule out dating a guy. But then the first chance he gets, he has to exchange fluids with Kenney."

"How many of us saw that coming?" I raise my hand.

"Oh, honey," Fred says. "Listen, I know you're just trying to make me feel better, but you haven't heard the worst part yet." He stands up and reaches down into the very long pocket of his very baggy pants. "When Kenney came by to tell me the news, she said I may as well return this to you on my way over here." He pulls a videotape out of his pocket and hands it to me.

And just as Fred is handing the tape to me, who else should come walking in?

My mother.

Did I say I was dead before? Because this time I really mean it.

I can feel my heart sliding into my shoes. It is heavy as a black rock, a lump of coal as slippery as silt.

# Meeting of the Minds

In the movie, there is a fast-forward moment of Neila and Fred running out of my house. Then cut to my mother with an overlaid image of a slow-motion, almost-still shot, of the atomic bomb exploding its brilliant colors and mushroom cloud of gold and blue and white and pink, and oh such brilliance and beauty in that one shining moment of disaster.

And here I am the next day, laying in my bed again, trying to read a magazine. Instead, all I can do is play moments of the past few days back through my head. A montage of scenes with Prudence grounding me for the rest of my life, Shawn laughing heartily at me, Henry tinkering in his basement and becoming ever more shadowy.

Then the part about the tape.

"Okay, have you seen it yet?" I ask Fred when he comes over. Prudence is at work, and we've all decided that as long as I'm grounded for the rest of my life anyway, we may as well meet at my house instead of the park.

"No," Fred says.

"But I assume you know what's on it?"

"She said it was you and Neila making out."

I turn my head so Fred can't see me smile. "Well, let's wait for Neila to get here so we can all find out together."

"Why am I involved in this?" Fred asks.

"Because you're a main character in my movie," I say. "And I want you here."

"Ready." Neila pops her head through the front door.

"Okay," I say. "Show time." My heart is thumping loudly against my rib cage as I press the *play* button.

We fast-forward through the part where we're talking about her room. Then her face gets bigger and blurrier and the camera cuts to the side. And the rest of the tape is one big long scene of the floor with the only sounds being quiet, muffled smooching and a bunch of giggling.

"That's it?" I say.

"Well, it's pretty obvious that you two are kissing," Fred says.

"Yeah," I say. "But it doesn't really look like any big deal."

"It's not like porn or anything," Neila says.

"Aren't you concerned at all?" Fred says.

"Why should we be?" Neila shrugs.

"What if Kenney tells everyone?" Fred says.

"What does it matter?" I ask. "No one ever bothers *you* about being gay."

"But," Fred says. "As far as they know, I'm not really gay. I mean, there's no proof I've ever made out with a guy."

"Grant has known about me for at least a year," Neila says. "And he hasn't been running around talking about his black lesbian cousin yet. It just isn't an issue."

"This isn't Grant we're talking about," Fred says. "I'm worried about Kenney."

"But she's Aurin's best friend," Neila says.

"Up until recently, anyway," Fred says.

"What are we going to do?" I ask. "Just sit around and wait for Kenney to call all the shots? I mean, she may be mad, but she isn't evil."

"Do you think she can keep a juicy bit of information like this to herself?" Fred asks.

"Good point," Neila says.

"So what if she tells everyone?" I ask. "We're living in the new millennium. This isn't the Stone Age, or even Ozzie and Harriet times."

"Aurin," Fred says. "Think about where we are. This is no cosmopolitan city, either."

"Oh, get over it, Fred," I say. "If this is one of your things about the North versus the South, you can forget it. Things are no different here than anywhere else."

"Maybe you have a point," he says. "People get beat up and harassed and killed everywhere, every day."

"Well, I'm not going to get killed," I say. "I thought it was you who said it wouldn't be so bad if I was gay."

"And I meant it," Fred says. "But I meant that it wouldn't be so bad for you to find out the truth about yourself. I didn't mean that it would be great for everyone else to know too."

"What's the difference?" I ask. "Honesty is honesty. Why would I want to lie to other people?"

"Why would you need to broadcast it?" Fred says.

"Why not?" I say. "You do."

Then Fred looks like I just slapped him. I didn't mean for this to become a big fight. I'm not particularly thrilled with the idea of losing *all* of my friends.

"Besides," Neila softens her voice, bridges the gap I've just made between Fred and me. "She's not broadcasting it. She's just not letting Kenney be in control over her fear."

"Fred," I say, "I'm sick of fighting with everybody. I need you to be my friend. We should all be glad about this." Then I adopt a plastic-y smile and the demeanor of a pleasant TV mom and say, "Just look in your thesaurus and you'll find another word for 'gay' is 'happy.'"

Fred laughs and nods. "I'm sorry," he says and gives me a hug.

"Me too," I say.

# Rub That Spot to Make It Clean

"What are you doing?" Pru is standing in my doorway. Fred and Neila left a few hours earlier, and I'm back to reading.

My head darts up from the magazine, snaps back to look at her. "Nothing."

She is still standing there.

"Reading." I hold up my magazine.

"Dinner's going to be ready soon." She stands there, leaning her head on the doorjamb, looking at me with one of those looks that doesn't know what it wants to be yet. She will not stop standing and staring.

"Okay," I say, to make her go away.

She is still there. She shifts her gaze upward and inspects the molding around the door, investigating the wood grain patterns. She runs her fingers along one group of swirls, tracing the pattern up along the edge. Notices a spot on the wall, picks at it with her fingernail, then wets her fingertip and tries rubbing the spot out. "So what's new with you?" she asks.

"Nothing."

She arches an eyebrow.

I shift my position, close the magazine, sit up. "What do you mean?" I ask.

"You are constantly depressed, you never talk to us anymore, you suddenly have a whole different group of friends . . ."

"I'm a teenager."

"You know honey, you can talk to us any time. If there's anything troubling you—" her voice is tight, stretched, strained— "and if it's your father and me that you don't feel comfortable talking with, I'm sure we can find someone else."

"Someone else?" I scrunch up my face. "Like *who*? A shrink?"

"There's nothing wrong with it." Prudence cocks her head to the side like a dog listening to a high-pitched sound. "Just for an extra person you would feel safe and comfortable talking to, if you need it."

"No," I say. "There *is* nothing wrong with it, but I feel plenty comfortable talking to people. And besides, my friends are not a whole different crowd."

She plays the innocent. "What about Kenney? It doesn't seem like she's so high on your list anymore. I thought you were best friends." Digging again at the spot on the wall. It's still there, and getting bigger, not unlike Fred's ink.

"Mom," I say, "people change."

She goes into my bathroom and pulls out a bottle of cleanser and a cleaning rag, comes back to the spot on the wall. "Mm-hmm," she says. "They do."

Well, *they* do, but *she* doesn't.

"And just who is it that has changed here, Aurin? Is it her? Or is it you?"

I take in a deep breath, let it out dramatically. "I don't know. Both of us, I guess."

Prudence is scrubbing, scrubbing. Shaking her head. "I don't think so," she says. "I think it's you. Kenney hasn't changed. She is still the same, delightful, clever young lady she has always

been. But you, on the other hand. You are mopey and make your-self miserable to be around."

"Miserable," I repeat-mumble. A flash of Neila's smile peeks into the corner of my brain. "You're right Mom." Neila laughing at me, holding her stomach she's laughing so hard, us laughing together until we have to roll onto our backs, exhausted, our cheeks stretched and sore. I can't help but smile now when I say this to her, "I'm the one who's changed."

"So why can't you go back to the way things were before?" Prudence says. "Just pull yourself together, apologize to Kenney."

"Apologize for what?"

"Well, you just said so yourself, you've changed." She's still scrubbing the wall, has moved on to more spots that need her attention.

"I'm not changing back, Mom. You think I'm like some kind of lizard or something that has a few colors in rotation and I can just get them back? I'm *growing up*, I'm not reversing time. And that isn't something I can apologize for."

"You know what I mean. Just be nicer, try to enjoy yourself. And stop hanging out with that Neil girl so much. The two of you make yourselves miserable together. I think she's dragging you down."

"Neila, Mom. Her name is Neila, not Neil. And I can't stop being her friend; I like her. And besides, all that has happened between Kenney and me is that we've grown apart. I've realized that she bosses me around too much and I don't like it." I shrug my shoulders like it's nothing. "Neila, on the other hand, treats me like a human being, not some dog of hers."

Still scrubbing the wall. She'll probably make a hole in it, or at least rub away the paint. "You don't have fun anymore," she says.

I laugh.

She stops scrubbing, drops her hand that is holding the rag to her side. "What?"

I shake my head, stifling the laugh. "I'm grounded," I say. "Remember?"

"You can't have fun here?"

"Sure, I can."

"No," Prudence shakes her head slowly back and forth. "I don't think you can. You sure haven't been. I haven't seen you have fun in quite some time. You used to have fun with Kenney."

"Yes," I say. "I did used to have fun with her. But now I don't. And I should be able to change friends. You used to say yourself that I didn't have enough friends. Now I have a new one, and you don't like that either. You won't acknowledge it. You can't even remember her name."

"This isn't about me, Aurin." Not scrubbing. Looking at me.

"It isn't?" I arch my eyebrows.

"Don't talk back to me." She's getting testy. "I'm your mother." She huffs off a little steam. I can see her getting wound up, but also fighting against that. Trying to get to the end of what she was meaning to say all along, without ruining it with her temper. She desperately *wants* to be a calmer mother, not so high-strung and tense when talking to her children. So here she is, standing in front of me with the rag in one hand, the bottle of cleanser in the other, and staring down at me from my doorway. And the whole reason she started this conversation in the first place is about something she's afraid of.

I look up at her, steel myself, wait for her to speak.

"I just want to know, what is so special about this new friend-ship? *Why* do you have so much fun together? What are you

doing that's so much better or different than with Kenney?"

I sit there, with my arms folded across my chest, look at her. I hold my gaze steady. "You wouldn't understand." I say this quietly, but not without force.

Prudence dips her head, averts her eyes from me, drops her shoulders slightly, places the cleanser and rag on the floor in front of my doorway. "I'm trying to." She is also quiet, though, in a weary way. She turns and goes downstairs, away from me.

# Origami Birds

So the past few days have been Walking on Eggshells with Pru. And I have to admit that at least two of those days have been Avoiding Kenney. And now there's today.

Since I'm still technically grounded, I have more than enough time on my hands. With my room immaculately clean by now, all that time leads to one thing: if anyone comes over without announcing it, they are likely to be greeted with a Frightening Thing. This thing would either be my face or hair. I might be trying to turn my incredibly brown hair into something more interesting like stripes, or I might be trying to turn my somewhat acne-disturbed face into a less disturbing one.

This happened today. I've got purple pomade streaks in my hair and am wearing an avocado mask to suck out the pimples and goo. Plus, I'm wearing the "alarming" orange dress that Pru hates. It has gigantic oval periwinkle spots with smaller hot pink blotches scattered about. Doorbell rings.

I don't go to answer it. Shawn is sitting in the living room. I run to my parents' room and look through their curtain. Kenney is shifting on the porch, looking back at the tree in our front yard. I dash to my bathroom and turn on the faucet.

Doorbell rings again.

"Hey, freaker," Shawn shouts to me, "can't you hear the doorbell?"

"Why don't you get it?" I yell back.

"You're not doin' nothin'."

I splash water on my face.

"It's her," he yells up the stairs at me. My friends don't get names from him. He can't be bothered to learn such mundane details, not even about people he's known for half my life. We're not people to him. We're specks of annoyance and inconvenience, unless we're momentarily worthy of harassment.

I'm scrubbing with my fingertips as quickly as possible, trying to remove all of the green mud.

A chill spreads up the back of my neck, and I know she's standing in my doorway. I turn off the water and quickly pat my face with a towel. And when I turn around, I'm right. She's standing there.

"Hey." Kenney's voice is quiet and a little shaky.

"Hi," I say.

"So."

"So."

We stand there for a moment and everything that isn't in my stomach because I haven't had lunch yet, and everything that is there because I did have breakfast, it all churns. Acidic burbles swelter and mix and change positions. The blood is draining out of my head, rushing down my neck, washing from my fingertips, receding.

Kenney places her hand on my wall as her knees dip slightly. The picture of my old best friend melting and rubbery.

Hot tears form under my bottom eyelids. My throat, even without the blood, swells. I take in a deep breath and let it out slowly, trying to stop myself from crying. "Okay," I whisper.

Kenney takes a shallower breath, and sucks her lips into her mouth, biting down.

"So I guess I haven't seen you in a couple of days," she says. She's holding something that looks like a coloring book.

"Yeah, I guess not," I say.

We're both still standing in our doorways at adjacent ends of my room.

"Can I come in?" she asks.

I nod. "Oh, um, yeah. Sure. Come on in." I motion for her to sit on my bed (the only real seat available). She sits on the floor, leans against my bed.

I walk over near her and sit on the floor, leaning against my closet door.

"I was thinking—have you ever tried origami?" she asks and puts the book on the floor beside her right foot.

"What?" She came over to talk about folding paper? Did I totally imagine we were fighting?

She fiddles with the book, sliding it back and forth on the carpet. "Its this thing where you . . ."

"I know what it is," I say.

"Oh. Right." She pauses, then puts on a falsely chipper-sounding voice. "Well, I got this book and some paper, and wanted to try it out, but didn't really have anyone to do it with."

"I'm sure you can do it alone." How rude I sound. I am surprising myself.

She's looking at the floor, sliding the book around. "But I also thought since I haven't seen you in a while, you might like to try it with me? I've always wanted to know how to make those paper cranes."

The Kenney I was used to before all this fighting would have never made origami birds with me. She is too cool for that. I am too cool not to. "Sure," I say. "Okay."

Her whole face sparks aglow into a variation of that flame I saw in her when we first met. "Really?" she asks. She kicks the book with her foot, by accident, while changing position. The book slides across my carpet and catches under the toe of my shoe. I pick it up and leaf through the pages.

"So what all can we make?" I ask.

"Well, there's boats and hats and footballs and cups and flowers and stuff. But I think the cranes are prettiest. And most frustrating probably, since they look so complicated."

Brilliant paper like a spray of peacock feathers fans out from the book. Metallic greens, blues, reds, and oranges. Antique yellow with Chinese red details. Soft Persian blue with golden flecks. Silky dusty purple with Phoenix-shaped watermarks.

"What if they look like shit?" I ask. "I don't want to mess up all your pretty paper."

"You won't," she says.

"What if I do?" I say.

"I won't care," she says. "We can unfold it and start over."

"Even if I fold it a million times wrong?"

"Then I can always get more."

"Maybe I'll get a practice sheet," I say and get up to grab a piece of notebook paper from my desk. "Hang on a sec," I say. Then I grab *Scrabble* from the hall closet so we can use the board for its surface.

"Good plan," Kenney says. She removes the fancy paper from the book and places it in a pile inside *Scrabble*'s box lid. She opens the book to the paper crane page. "So what have you been up to these days?" she asks.

"Oh, the usual, I guess," I say. I fold my notebook paper into a right triangle.

"Really? And what's that?" She folds her paper the same way.

I feel like I'm on a job interview, where the position I'm applying for is Kenney's friend. And I'm not sure yet whether or not I want the job again because I don't know what my duties will entail this time.

"Just hanging out, I guess," I say. I fold the extra edge of paper over. "What about you?" I carefully tear the edge off that makes my paper into a square.

"Oh, me?" she asks. Her paper is already a square. "I went to dance class. Didn't see you there. Were you sick?"

"Grounded," I say. I look at the directions in the book.

"Yeah. I guess people don't get sick too often in the summer," she says. Her folds are a step or two ahead of mine. "Unless it's heat sickness. That happens a lot."

"Yeah," I say. "I'm really sensitive to heat." I fold the paper, but realize that I've folded it in the wrong direction.

"Maybe you should drink more water," she says. "That usually helps."

I unfold my paper and start over. "I guess there's been something else too," I say.

She stops folding. "Oh, really? What's that?"

I refold my paper in the right direction and catch up to where she is. "I think you might know."

Her hands are shaking a little. She tries to pick up her paper, but her fingers slide along the *Scrabble* board. "Yeah," she says. "I think I might."

I fold my paper a few more creases. "Do you think you might want to talk about it?" My notebook paper is almost a bird. Hers is still a bunch of triangles.

"I might," she says. She folds hers a few more creases so that it now looks like mine. "I guess that's partly why I came over here today.

"Okay," I say. I pull out a sliver of paper and fold down the head, then tug out the tail, and bend down the wings.

I hold up my bird. "Let's talk."

Kenney moves over to sit next to me and she pulls down the beak and wings of her bird.

We're silent for a while, and continue making birds while I wait for her to talk.

"There are some things," Kenney says, "that I don't have to know about my friends until they are ready to tell me. And I will still love them, even if I do get mad."

I am surprised to be hearing this come from her. It sounds like a large admission, like it's difficult for her to say.

We both look down at the metallic paper birds scattered around our feet, each carefully folded along its creases. They are flames and stars in brilliant hues.

"Me too," I say.

Kenney buries her fingers in the carpet, combs through it, leaves rake marks, then smooths over it again. Like sand. She assembles the birds in a row, arranges them in color order. When she looks up at me, her eyes look tired, but show a small glint of their sparkle.

"We better do something with all these birds," I say.

"You got any thumbtacks?" she asks.

A smile spreads across my face. "Yeah," I say. I reach into my desk drawer and pull out the tacks and scissors and invisible thread.

"Okay then." Kenney starts cutting lengths of thread and stringing them through the birds. She hands them to me, each attached to a thumbtack.

I stand on a chair and carefully hang each bird from its invisible thread, suspended from the ceiling.

*Tea Benduhn*

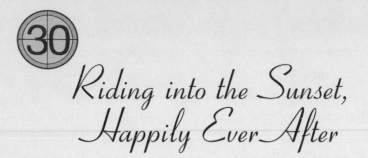

# Riding into the Sunset, Happily Ever After

At the end of my movie, we will all be there: Prudence, Henry, and Shawn. Kenney, Grant, Fred, and Neila. I want to say that we're riding off into the sunset because late afternoons are perfect for endings, and also in order to make it a completely round movie that refers back to the beginning. But there won't be anything for us to ride on and there won't be anywhere for us to *go*. Especially since we never really went anywhere anyway. I mean, we were in Greensboring the whole time. And on top of that, nothing even really *happened*.

Or maybe everything did.

The end of my movie will be a big dance scene by the lake. We will all be looking glamorous in our '40s clothes and hair. Even me.

My mom will be played by Lisa Kudrow (of course, she'll have to be made up to look older) and my dad by Bill Murray. She will be gazing lovingly into his eyes. Smiling at Neila. Smiling at me.

And because I want life to be like this, Fred will be dancing with Grant. And it'll turn out that Fred has mastered the dance moves from class and is the most graceful one on the floor. He's found a genuine flair for it. He's sweeping Grant along and they almost look like they're swimming.

Since Kenney has to have a dance partner, Shawn will have to climb down from his imaginary pedestal of cool. It strikes me that

I should have thought of this before—they'd be great together. But for the sake of the movie, he merely acts as a prop for Kenney's beautiful gloriousness. She glows in the center, a red flame.

Until the camera sweeps the floor, pushing Kenney and Shawn into the corner, and pans to Neila and me. Just for the hell of it, we're wearing pink taffeta dresses with our hair all done up, almost like prom. Each of us wears a piece of gravel tied to a string around our throats. And I don't even need to pee because we're dancing together and we are perfect.

Kenney looks over Shawn's shoulder and smiles at me. I look over Neila's and wink back at her. We are definitely best friends again. Forever. In the movie.

We're in a large gazebo-like pavilion by the lake. All of our favorite foods are there: ice cream and tofu. Scratch and that guy are playing music in the background that we're dancing to. They're singing:

*Every summer she plucked discarded wings*
*from the bushes, untangling them from leaves.*
*She placed them on her tongue, bits of flame*
*like communion wafers, swallowing them whole.*
*Those wings lined her belly and spun cocoons*
*until she grew more into the shape of the sun*
*and released the butterflies one by one.*

And unlike the community arts center, this time there really is a glittery shine to the air, alluding to the disappointing crud of before. And we're so pretty, every one of us. And all in place and all in desperate, mad, comfortable, gorgeous love. Ridiculously happy but in a way that seems like it's genuine and that it'll last. Because this is *my* movie.

Camera pans to Neila giving me butterfly kisses with her eyelashes on my eyelids. She does something that looks like holding her hand over her heart, cupping it in her palm, and giving it to me. Maybe she says, "Here, I have something for you." Or maybe she picks it up from the gravel and gives it to me.

Happily ever after, and all of that.

And off into the bursting exploding sunset.

And then all of a sudden I realize that I haven't been breathing for quite some time. I've been holding my breath underwater through the whole thing, waiting for something big and important to happen, when in reality it all just seemed so normal. It seemed like my life just fell into the place that it did, and I can't even remember the point I was trying to make with it.

All of this water that I've been under—it's been air the whole time. And this gravel I'm standing on is solid and sturdy.

Camera pans out as a breeze swooshes in and blows around our hair and dresses. A flutter of colorful paper gets stirred up. The wind lifts the pile and releases a thousand paper metallic origami birds. They're bursting into flight all through the sky.